SLEEPING WITNESS

Bryan Moore

BRYAN MOORE is an accountant by profession, though he entered the Army in his youth and spent time on the staff of Sandhurst, the UK's major officer-training college.

He originated and related stories to his children, and in 1993 he collated these into a children's book. In the same year, his first poem was included in a National Library of America's publication. A few years later, Shelagh Nugent published his first short story. Since then, many of his poems and short stories have appeared in print.

When his pen is not conjuring up a set of accounts or even a few murders here and there, he takes on the guise of the lazy man's Bill Oddie, by studying a variety of bird-life and animal life in his own back garden.

Prologue

Both the portal and hall of the State Union Bank were impressive. A large statue filled the entrance and no customer could overlook the fact that it was an all-American bank. Further along, a fountain was set at the rear of a marble-pillared and open-paved area. It squirted its jets of water in various sequences through numerous outlets in an artistic display without a single drop landing on the floor or on any member of the public. The President of the Bank called it a suitable accompaniment to the business conducted on the premises by the Bank and its customers. And according to the Bank, the general public agreed. At least those with children did as it kept their little dears amused whilst their parents or guardians were otherwise engaged.

A range of counters faced the concourse and on a particular day, two men were standing in line for one of the counters. The man in front was short and podgy and the other immediately behind him was of similar height and known by his companion as "the tank". He carried a small briefcase in his hand, and when the last customer moved aside, he used it to give his companion a purposeful prod in the back. It sent him lurching forward temporarily flattening his protruding stomach against the counter. He grinned sheepishly at the young female teller behind it, though she was too busy moving papers around to notice. With a smirk, the tank withdrew and headed for one of the bank's leather-upholstered seats. His companion gathered himself up and announced:

'I wish to open an account with a large certified cheque.' The teller beamed back at him across the counter.

'Certainly, sir! If you could let me know your name, I'll arrange a meeting with one of our senior managers right away.' He gave her his name and she copied it down on a piece of paper.

'Nice to welcome you to the State Union,' she responded warmly. 'If you'll please take a seat, our Mr Barton will be with you shortly.'

He thanked her and seated himself next to the tank, whereupon the tank withdrew a passport from the briefcase and placed it in his companion's hand with instructions to study it in detail. Once he'd done so and it was safely back inside the briefcase, the case was passed over to the companion with a reminder as to the importance of the visit. To emphasise the point, the tank gave the fingers of the man's left hand a long, hard squeeze. The tank knew he was right-handed and assured him that in time his fingers would return to normal. Under such circumstances, the companion could be excused for not noticing a woman standing a few feet away to one side of him. She recognised him instantly but before she could open her mouth, Mr Barton appeared with a breezy 'Hi!' He invited the prospective customer to come into his office, not forgetting to add the customer's name.

On hearing it, the woman froze. Gingerly placing the briefcase under his left arm with his damaged fingers extended straight down the side of his trouser leg, he raised his right hand for a handshake and was ushered through a large mahogany and reeded-glass door into a plush office set behind the bank of tellers.

The woman continued to stare after him in disbelief.
The names of the characters have been changed to mask their true identities. And within America's Pacific Northwest and its surrounds, place names have been changed to fictitious ones instead. The tale may be based on fact, but the Pentagon's involvement should be treated as fiction.

As G. K. Chesterton put it: "fiction is a necessity"...at least it is in this case.

Chapter One

Nathaniel Foskett trudged round the lake. Although still in his thirties, his lack of height accentuated the look of his portly figure. American ladies described him as cuddly. An embarrassment, as it was the unattractive ones who insisted on clasping him to their bosoms. As a chartered accountant, a tax consultant and a financial adviser, he considered exercise of the brain to be of far greater importance than exercise of the body. But as today was a free day, he'd been advised by his client, Warren Tate, a property dealer and local big-wig, that the other side of the lake was well worth a visit and that he should get over there and sweat off a few surplus pounds on the way. Even though Nat was never at a loss for words (an adviser's natural forte), he couldn't come up with an acceptable excuse.

At his normal pace, it took him quite a while to locate the alleged beauty spot, but it needed no more than a cursory inspection of his surroundings to conclude that a horizontal position might serve him best. He stretched himself out on the lush grass and rested his mass of dark brown hair upon it. He focused his greyish-green eyes on the cloudless, bright-blue sky above. He could hear the water gently lapping the bank, intermingled with the constant buzz of hummingbirds. A meadowlark burst into song, sweet, soothing and so restful.

Perfect, he thought. How good it felt to be alive.

His eyes closed and his mind drifted into space. For a moment, he was conscious of the sound of distant voices, but only for a moment.

Cra-a-ack!

Nat stirred, mumbled, and slumbered on.

Chapter Two

Set in a forest of ponderosa pines at the edge of the Calghooie National Park, Roseacre Retirement Retreat nestled on the side of a hill overlooking the township of Spiros...a peaceful and idyllic setting, and for many, a perfect home for the elderly. Though for Sheriff Oswald Kramer things were far from perfect. He was beginning to find his regular trips to Roseacre quite a bind. At first, Roseacre seemed to be an ideal home for his mother also. She'd spent all her married life in Spiros with her late husband and so she imagined (rather optimistically as it turned out) that life would continue much in the same vein after his death. Unfortunately, Oswald was obliged to live near his work in Moose City. There was nothing he could do about it. It was a fact of life. But the old woman could never see it that way. She'd grown bitter with age and to make matters worse, she'd partially lost the use of one of her legs. It had reached the stage where his visits were never appreciated and no matter how hard he'd pleaded with her, his mother refused to budge from the vicinity of Spiros and from her memories of happier bygone days.

As usual, he'd brought along her favourite chocolates and flowers, yet, although they were accepted as part and parcel of her son's visit, they inevitably failed to please. The nursing staff put it down to frustration due to her general infirmity. Apparently she was as good as gold during the rest of the month. Bringing his daughter, Ermentrude, along with him helped no end. The animosity was far less prominent and the four-letter words hardly evident. With a bunch of mixed carnations in one hand and a box of soft-centred chocolates in the other, Oswald opened the door of her room apprehensively and entered. Ermentrude followed on, carrying a scarf and a bottle of rye.

At twenty-two, Erm (as she was affectionately called) was tall, with a head of golden hair and the deepest of blue eyes. Her ample proportions attracted many a long, lustful look from the young men in the area. But that's as far as it went. She saw to it that nobody messed with her. She could take on any man or woman and beat them into submission without drawing breath. As a law enforcement officer herself, Erm was keen to prove her worth. Although her ultimate goal was to become a detective of some repute, for the time being she was proud to act as her father's 'right-hand man'. And the Sheriff was more than happy to have an assistant he could rely on.

Gran had complained of a pain in the neck. Oswald had complained of a similar condition. So the scarf was for gran and the rye was for her father. The old woman was seated in a wicker chair next to the bed. As he appeared in the doorway, she eyed her son up and down critically, all six foot, six inches of him, from his size eleven boots to the top of his balding head.

'Why're-you late?' on spotting her granddaughter, a trace of a smile creased her lips.

The Sheriff held out his gifts for inspection.

'We're not late, ma.'

Erm wrapped the scarf around the old woman's neck.

'Put the flowers in water, there's a good girl.'

She pointed to a vase on a shelf.

Erm dutifully obliged and inquired as to her grandmother's present state of health. But gran was too preoccupied with the box of chocolates to consider it. She tore the wrappings apart and dumped them bit by bit into Erm's outstretched hands for her to consign to the waste-paper bin. As gran finally managed to raise the lid of the box, she eyed the contents with a look of triumph. This was swiftly followed by a look of pleasure as she crammed her mouth full.

The Sheriff also inquired as to his mother's state of health but was no more successful than his daughter. They both sat on the bed and awaited a response. It came during her attempt to consume the second layer.

'I'm not well.'

Erm whispered into her father's ear: 'Who would be, after gorging all those chocs?'

Gran was about to elaborate, when the phone rang.

'Answer it, Erm. Me hands just ain't good enough to hold a phone.'

Though, Erm reflected, they were good enough to hold a box of chocolates.

Erm lifted the receiver. 'Yeah! The Sheriff's here,' she passed the phone on to him. 'It's an emergency, pop.'

The thought of it came as a welcome respite.

'Is that you, Connor?'

Connor Quigley was the Deputy Sheriff, pro tem, and his long held ambition was to make the position permanent. Accordingly, he milked his expert handling of the situation for all it was worth.

'You've caught the bastard?'

A long explanation followed, meaning: Yes, he had.

'You've found the murder weapon?'

Another long explanation followed, again meaning: Yes, he had.

'You've done well, Connor,' Connor knew it.' We'll be back as soon as we can. The drive will take a couple of hours. Check the weapon for dabs and with ballistics.'

'It's all in hand,' replied Connor.

Oswald put the phone down.

'What's up?' Erm stared at her father anxiously.

'There's been a fatality,' he leaned over his mother. 'Got to go now, ma.'

'Already? Just as well I've got a carer who cares.'

'Duty calls!'

'Duty? At least my carer knows what the damn word means.'

'But someone's been shot, ma. I've got to go. You must see that. And before you know it, we'll be back together again this time next month.'

'Sooner than that, son. The carer's visiting her brother in Moose City next week and says she'll drop me off at your place on the way. She'll collect me on her way back later in the day. I told her not to go to any trouble, but she insists. She's sure the trip will do me a power of good.'

The Sheriff doubted it but kept his mouth shut.

Though once outside, he let rip.

'Damn carers! Why the hell can't they mind their own business?'

The drive back gave him plenty of time to cool down. Before long, homicide (a rare event in Moose City) was fully occupying his mind, though it dampened the two's normal father and daughter banter to no more than a few words.

'Warren Tate...dead?' Erm's voice was one of disbelief.

'So Connor says. And what's even harder to credit, he reckons it's the Brit who killed him. Let's hope Connor's got it right for once.'

'Amen to that. I'm still holding your bottle of rye, pop.'

'Amen, to that, too.'

The remainder of the journey passed in silence, except for the sound emanating from Oswald's gullet when a finger or two of the rye slid down it. He carried his liquor well. If anything it seemed to improve his concentration. So when at last he and Erm stepped into the Sheriff's Office in Moose City, he was feeling as sharp as a needle.

'What's the latest, Connor?'

'The boys from ballistics are checking the bullet. The rifle's a Gibbs Parker-Hale 85 with scope. High precision. A beaut. It's been wiped clean though.'

'Pity! As soon as we know it's the murder weapon, you and Elmer can check around to see if it's been bought legit, though I doubt it.'

'Will do.'

'They say, pop, that a Gibbs 85 can part your hair at six hundred yards.'

Oswald patted his bald patch with amusement. 'Present company excepted, Erm.'

'Natch!' she replied, though her eyes were glued on Connor. 'Where did you find it?'

'We found it on the other side of the lake, half hidden, next to the Limey, Foskett.'

'Who's "we"?'

'Well, it was Elmer who found the rifle. He called me over to make the arrest in case there was any trouble.'

Elmer Ezekiah shuffled his feet and smiled superciliously. He was an officer noted for his dogged devotion to duty and low IQ.

'OK!' The Sheriff nodded approvingly. 'Where's Foskett now?'

'Safe in the cell, Oswald. I put him there peaceful enough at first, but afterwards, he made a hell of a fuss. Says he wants a lawyer. Says he's going to sue us, too.' Connor laughed derisively. 'As if he could?'

'How did it happen?'

The acting Deputy Sheriff leaned back in his chair and plonked his cowhide-booted feet firmly across the table.

'Tate was shot as he stood on the jetty,' he said, 'plumb through the heart. He was facing the lake at the time.' Connor stopped for a moment to cross his legs and shift his bulk into a more comfortable position. 'I sent Elmer out to take a recce round the lake to see if he could spot anything, the murder weapon, or at least some idea of its whereabouts.' He placed his hands at the back of his head and stuck out his chest with pride. 'We found 'em both, the weapon and the murdering bastard.'

'And what was Foskett doing at the time? Was he just waiting around to be arrested?'

'Snoring!' Elmer beamed at the Sheriff.

'What-d'you mean...*snoring*?'

'His snores hit me as soon as I reached the track on the left side of the lake. It was quiet there, away from Annie. She was bawling her head off on the path by the jetty and they were doing their darnedest to shush her up.'

'No! No!' said Connor. 'The Doc and the others were trying to console her, not shush her up.'

'Well's the same thing, ain't it?'

Oswald was aware of the fact that Annie Tate was spending a few weeks at her uncle's estate in Fortuna Valley. On the occasions they'd met, he'd found her intelligent, pleasant and chatty (if a touch on the emotional side) and the kind of girl unlikely to ever go unnoticed. Her striking copper, flowing locks and emerald-green eyes combined with a perfect figure saw to that. She tended to visit Warren on a regular basis in order (as he put it) to add charm and beauty to his drab life. Although at thirty-four he was fifteen years her senior, Oswald could see how much Warren enjoyed having her around and how much she enjoyed his hospitality. Each and every day, Annie would wallow in her most cherished pursuits, gourmet delights coupled with a minimum of activity. Amazingly, neither had had any detrimental effect on her figure.

'Let me get this straight.' Oswald's steely-grey eyes bore down on Connor. 'When you arrived at the lake, was the suspect still flaked out on the ground?'

'Yep.'

'So you reckon he used the rifle to kill Tate, cleaned off his dabs, and left it lying around.'

'It was propped up against a tree,' Elmer called out.

'Thanks, Elmer...by a tree. And then as he was feeling a mite bushed having had his work cut out carrying the darn thing around with him, he got a mind to stretch out on the grass for a siesta. Is that about the size of it? Is that what you think happened, Connor?'

'I guess so. Who knows how a murderer's mind works?'

'Well you don't, that's for sure. And another thing, how do you know Tate was facing the lake when he was shot?'

'Annie said so.'

'Was Annie on the jetty at the time?'

'She was having a picnic on the other side of the lake, the same side as where we found Foskett, but near the end by the freeway.'

'A picnic?' Sheriff Kramer looked at his daughter with astonishment. 'That's not like her.'

'What-d'you mean, pop?'

'You know Annie. Food alfresco just ain't her scene.'

'Be that as it may,' Connor's voice rose in a show of irritation. 'That's what she said. She spotted Tate across the lake standing on the jetty. She was waving and calling out to him, friendly like, and he was waving and calling back to her when it happened. It fair shook her up, I can tell you.'

'Be that as it may,' with a hint of sarcasm, Oswald mimicked Connor. 'I still can't figure out what Annie was doing over there? Was she on her own or was she with someone?'

'She was with Bennett. They were having the picnic together.'
Erm's eyes twinkled mischievously.

'I bet that's not all they were having together.'

'What-d'you mean?' Connor eyed her up and down. 'Bennett's the chauffeur, ain't he? His job is to drive the limo, ain't it? And that's what he did. What's wrong with that?'

'There's nothing wrong with that, Connor.' The Sheriff nodded in agreement. 'Erm's fooling around. She knows that Annie fancies Bennett.'

'OK, pop. And Bennett fancies her. I reckon it could be significant.'

'It could be,' though the look on his face suggested he thought otherwise.

'And what about the suspect?' Erm's question was directed at Connor.

'What about him?'

'You said he came quietly but cut up rough later. What made him do that?'

'That's easy, Erm.' Elmer was only too willing to inform her. 'D'you know, that guy Foskett's got letters after his name. S'posed to be a clever bastard. But we know differently, don't we Connor? He's plain dumb.' He guffawed fit to burst. 'Can you credit it? He thought he was being booked for a traffic offence.'

The Sheriff exploded.

'He thought...*what*?'

Connor gesticulated for all his worth for Elmer to shut up, but to no avail.

'If anything, I guess it was more of a parking offence. And then when he found out it weren't, he blew his top. Can you believe it?'

'No, Elmer, I darn-well can't,' the Sheriff glared menacingly at Connor. 'You said you went over to help Elmer make the arrest. Didn't you tell Foskett why he was being arrested?'

Connor uncrossed his boots and stuck a nervous finger along the inside of his collar. A few beads of sweat appeared on his brow and began to multiply. They trickled down his cheek. He pulled himself up in his seat and tried his best to put on a brave face.

'I . . . I kind of thought there'd be less aggro, if I didn't mention it, not at first, you see. Not straightaway. Put him under pressure. Try and catch him out. I mean to say, Oswald, given time, I guess he was sure to cave in, don't you think?'

'No, I don't think...and neither it seems do you,' the Sheriff leaned over him eyeball to eyeball. 'Tell me, Connor, what gave him the goddamn notion he'd committed a traffic offence? And it better be good.'

'Yesterday, he had the nerve to park his car on our parking lot in *my* space.'

'So what? If we know 'em we let 'em park there, don't we?'

'That's true, Oswald. But we don't know *him*. He ain't Stars and Stripes.'

Erm stared at him aghast.

'What's that got to do with it? In any case, I let him park there. He asked me, real nice, too, polite-like. I can tell you, he sure acts better than most guys around here. He is a gen-u-ine gentleman.'

It was Connor's turn to look aghast. 'Why did you have to put him in my space?'

'Didn't you tell me you'd be late back? I went out on patrol with Elmer, so how d'you expect me to figure out you were going to change your mind? Anyhow, my space was available.'

'That's not the point.'

As the Sheriff's eyes descended again, they were drawn like a magnet to Connor's boots still resting nonchalantly across the desk. At one fell swoop, he grabbed their leather buckles and yanked his legs high in the air.

'Now get off your butt,' he bawled, 'and go and release the suspect... *pronto!*'

Connor's feet clattered to the floor followed swiftly by his abject body.

'And when you've done that...' In an instance, the acting Deputy Sheriff scrambled to his feet and legged it to the cell. Oswald's voice rose to a crescendo, 'put him in my office. Erm can see to him. And you can spend your time phoning ballistics to find out the score. And if it is the murder weapon - and for your sake you'd better pray it is - you and Elmer can spend the rest of the day trying to trace its source. Got it!'

Erm stared at her father in horror.

'You want *me* to see to him?'

'Sure do.'

'But why me, pop?'

''Cos you're the only one I can trust to do a good job,' to help reassure his daughter, the Sheriff placed an arm around her shoulder. 'Unless you think otherwise, I reckon Foskett's in the clear. And if that proves to be the case, the best we can hope for is if he saw or heard something helpful before he flaked out.'

'I agree! I can't see Nat being the killer.'

'Nat?' the Sheriff withdrew his arm and stared at her questioningly. 'You know him well enough to call him that?'

Erm eyed her father up and down. 'I guess he did chat me up, but it was all proper-like, you know. The local car park was full and I couldn't let him park in the street.'

'Not with them NO PARKING signs, you couldn't.'

'Nat has an Irish-American mom, just like me, though *his* pop's English. And his mom wears the trousers, just like...' her voice tailed off.

'You mean like gran when grandpa was around?'

'Yeah, her an' all. That's why Nat works over here. Trouble is I'm not too sure I can do it.'

'Do what?'

'Interrogate him.'

The Sheriff scowled disapprovingly.

'Not interrogate, Erm. We're in enough trouble as it is,' he again placed an arm around his daughter's shoulder and stared anxiously into her eyes. 'After Connor's spectacular screw-up, as things stand Foskett's not likely to give us much in the way of co-operation. The idea is for you to ease him out nice and cool-like so he'll be more willing to open up.'

'And what-d'you think I should do to ease him out?'

'Let him think you fancy him.'

'As it happens, I think he's OK.'

'No problem then.'

As she spun round to enter her father's inner sanctum, she added under her breath: 'Except for one. Who's going to ease me out?' Connor had seated Nat in front of the Sheriff's desk. Erm gave him a warm and welcoming smile, though her heart was pounding away nineteen to the dozen. And she couldn't quite figure out the reason why. Could it be to do with Nat's proximity? Although his manners were a big plus, he didn't really look like the kind of guy she would even give a first glance to, let alone allow him to fill her eyeballs for a second time. Though without saying or doing anything, he seemed to possess an attraction she couldn't readily define. She reckoned his presence might be at least a contributory factor in helping to raise her temperature. On the other hand, as likely as not, it was probably due to her present assignment. But whichever it was, she knew the time had come for officer Ermentrude Kramer to undertake the most important investigation of her career.

However, if anything her initial words somewhat belittled the significance of the occasion.

'PQ?' she exclaimed. 'Hang on a goddamn minute, Nat?'

A quizzical frown wrinkled her smooth, white brow as she charged back to the doorway and stuck her head out.

'What are you going to be doing, pop, whilst I'm in here?'

'Me? Getting something urgent from outside to help keep my mind focused on the case inside.'

'What's of help outside?'

'It's in the car.'

'You mean...?'

'Yeah! That bottle of rye.'

'It doesn't always help, pop.'

'Maybe not...but I guess it's *always* worth a try.'

Chapter Three

Warren Tate's imposing residence stood high above the water, shrouded by a pinetum interspersed with immaculate lawns, fancy walls, a lavishly paved area surrounding an equally lavish swimming pool, and walkways edged by numerous exotic plants and shrubs. A path led down to the jetty and to the boathouse beside it. Woods and grassland surrounded the lake, where kingfishers and blue herons nested near the shore and a variety of ducks hid themselves in the reeds and bulrushes. The lake was over half a mile in length and, at one end, a third of a mile in width. By the time it passed the outfall from the Big Rock River and reached the point where the freeway swept around the water's edge, it had narrowed to almost half in size. And on its journey from the mountains of Big Rock, the river skipped and splashed over numerous large boulders shaped smooth in the course of time by the precipitation of water as it plummeted down a series of rapids. Once it had run out of steam, it took a more leisurely course via the outskirts of the metropolis of Fort Jackson and on through the township of Moose City, eventually descending further to snake majestically in and out of the lake through the lower valley of Fortuna. And it was around this lake that Nathaniel Foskett found himself once more experiencing the benefits (or otherwise) of physical exercise. It seemed to him unprecedented in the extreme that this selfsame pursuit could have arisen within a period of less than twenty-four hours. And to make matters worse, within that short period of time, everything that could have gone wrong had bloody well gone wrong.

Warren Tate, his client and host, was killed by a bullet from a rifle dumped near to where he'd been resting by the edge of the lake. In addition, he'd suffered the indignity of being arrested as the prime suspect and Annie, his epicurean soul mate and young friend (or so he thought), had told him in no uncertain manner to hit the road and never darken the Tate's Fortuna Valley doorway again.

There he was, one day living in the lap of luxury and the next day he was living in the Most Welcome Motel, bereft of baths and French cuisine. In stark contrast, it excelled in unworkable showers and fast food. On the other hand, his current companion truly epitomised the words, "most welcome". Erm alone could boost his ego, being the only bright star shining out of his current desolate firmament.

She was dressed in civvies and not in her usual grey, dowdy uniform. Even better, her rig-out couldn't fail to catch the eye, being a bright hug-me-tight blouse and skirt. But after awhile, no amount of chatting could raise in her a response of any sort. Admittedly, Warren's death had depressed him no end. But now it looked as if it was affecting Erm as well. And why it should was a puzzle. She'd disappeared into her shell and no matter how hard he tried, she refused to let him coax her out of it. Earlier on, she'd been very lively and chatty, especially when he disclosed to her what he'd heard on his previous excursion round the lake...the sound of gunshot. One shot fired and from not that far away either. Unfortunately, her enthusiasm took a bit of a nosedive once she realised the gun was fired up to half an hour before the murder took place. They agreed it was probably a hunter. And Nat was continuing to mull over the matter when the hairs on the back of his neck stiffened up like a porcupine's quills. Caught in mid-stride, he stumbled back against the parapet suspended high above the Big Rock River. He stared into space feeling as if someone was walking over his grave.

Erm peered at him with a degree of concern.

'Aren't you feeling well?'

'I'm OK, thanks. It's the footbridge.'

'You're not keen on heights?'

'No... I mean, yes. I mean it doesn't bother me one way or the other.'

As he gazed into her eyes, a voice within him compelled him to look beyond her. In the distance he could see the water cascading and twinkling in the rays of the sun. It tumbled and splashed against the side of the bank in its attempt to negotiate the bend at the edge of the lake a hundred yards or so upstream. Somehow he knew it was nothing to do with the water. He stretched out an arm and pointed to the opposite bank at the point where the lake and river merged into one.

'I've got it, Erm!' he was bubbling fit to burst. 'There was somebody over there.'

Erm spun round and followed the direction of his finger across the water. 'D'you mean to say that when you passed by here yesterday, you actually *saw* someone on the other side of the river?'

'I did! He was standing in that clearing in the trees.'

'What did he look like?'

'He was wearing a baseball cap and when he twigged I'd cottoned on to him, he ducked down out of sight. At the time, I thought nothing of it. It wasn't of any interest then. In fact, it'd slipped my memory altogether.'

'Did you notice anything else about him?'

'Apart from the cap, there wasn't much else to notice. It was casting a shadow over his face. Even so, I'm sure he was white. I only saw him for a few seconds, though come to think of it, he did seem sort of familiar. I felt I knew him from somewhere. But it couldn't have been anyone from the house.'

'What makes you think that?'

'I'm pretty certain it wasn't the security guard, Craig, and it couldn't have been Bennett. He's black and was with Annie at the time. And it couldn't have been Warren's gardener-cum-handyman, Oliver. Earlier on, Warren was moaning about being left short-handed. Apparently, he'd lost Oliver's services due to the fact that he'd had to depart on a mission of mercy to an elderly aunt in Fort Jackson. She'd suffered a fall or something and was in urgent need of tender LC.'

'Tender Elsie! Who-the-hell is she?'

'Not Elsie...*L-C*! Loving Care. Don't you have that in America?'

'Sure thing! Pop's into that kind of stuff with gran, except he doesn't care much for those who do and the loving is fairly well hidden as well.'

'As was our mystery man.'

'Then who could it be?'

Nat grimaced and shook his head.

'Sorry, I can't think who or where for that matter. But that raises an interesting question. As there's only one path from this point onwards and as I didn't pass him on my way, how did our mystery man manage to disappear?'

'Not into thin air, that's for sure.'

'But if he disappeared into the woods - and from here onwards, the density of the trees and undergrowth would be a bit off-putting to say the least - why should anybody want to deviate from the path unless he didn't want to be seen?'

'Or be recognised?'

'That too.'

'And as far as I can tell that clearing looks like the only open space facing the bridge on either side of the river, up or downstream,' Nat gave the river's wooded banks a long hard look both ways before giving her the nod. 'We can check on it when we get there,' Erm went on, 'I reckon someone standing on that exact spot could not only see the bridge and anyone attempting to cross it, but if that someone turned and looked the other way, I'm willing to bet a fistful of our dollars to one of your British pounds that he would find the jetty and the other side of the lake well within his sights.'

'Do you suppose it was the gunman himself I saw?'

'I reckon it's more than likely. A bullet from that rifle could easily have covered the distance. Mind you, to be able to hit Tate at that kind of distance means the gunman has to be a hell of a good shot,' they turned to complete the walk over the bridge. But Erm could only manage a few strides. 'I can't,' she screeched. 'I can't stand it any more. My skirt is damn-well killing me.'

Her outburst stopped Nat in his tracks and changed his face to one of compassion. He, too, had bought clothes (even from the most reputable of tailors) where although the tag clearly showed his correct size, it often turned out not to be the case.

'You should have complained and returned it to the shop.'

'You don't understand. I haven't worn a skirt for ages. As pop reckoned plain clothes would be less conspicuous on our walk, I thought I'd try out one of my old ones.'

'Old or not, it's still outrageous.'

'Forget it, will you? My problem's here and now.'

'But that's not a problem,' Nat rummaged through his pockets. 'Rescue is at hand. Like a true Boy Scout, an accountant must be prepared at all times,' he produced a safety pin and held it triumphantly aloft.

She couldn't quite figure out whether it was a try-on or not. But as the pain was close to unbearable, she decided to throw caution to the wind. With a sigh of relief, she unzipped her skirt and held it in position around her waist.

'You pin it up at the back. If I do it, chances are I'll stab myself in the butt,' Nat agreed in a flash. Though it took longer than expected. The allotted task was having an adverse effect on the synchronisation of his brain's instructions to his fingers as to the movements required. No matter what, he just couldn't stop them shaking. Over her shoulder, Erm gave him an appreciative smile. 'D'you know, in the past when I wore a skirt, most guys I met encouraged me to take it off. You're the first one I've come across to act keen-like for me to keep it on.'

Nat eyed the back of her head with mixed feelings. Was this an insult or a compliment? 'I'm always willing to help a lady in distress,' he told her. He considered the number of attractive young women who'd sought his aid in the past - he failed to come up with a single one.

They continued across the bridge and along the path until they reached the clearing in the trees. This is it, Nat thought to himself. A good view of the jetty and of the victim standing on it and away from where he'd slept yet close enough to dump the murder weapon nearby afterwards. On the other hand, why on earth take the added risk of going out of his way when all the main access routes were in the opposite direction?

'To be honest, I'm beginning to dislike our murderer over and above the fact that he killed my client.'

'*Our* murderer?'

'I appreciate that as the officer investigating the case, it's your problem, but for some peculiar reason, it feels as if it's my problem as well,' as he spoke, he spotted something on the ground. With a hand firmly placed on the trunk of a tree for support, he bent over enough to take a closer look behind it. 'Footprints!' he called out to her. 'They look fairly fresh ones to me.'

'Hold your horses,' she called back. 'Don't touch a thing. Step away and let me give pop a ring.'

It turned out that both the Sheriff and his acting Deputy were engaged with the Deputy Sheriff of Fort Jackson and with representatives of the Federal Bureau of Investigation. And when she asked what was going on, Elmer hadn't a clue. But until she knew the score, all she could do was to wait and trust Elmer to pass on the message.

She spelt it out to him.

'Now remember what I've told you,' she said. 'Tell pop we've found footprints by the path round the lake and we need the lab guys from Fort Jackson to check 'em out. And tell him about the other shot fired yesterday. Get him to call me back, if you can. OK?'

'Yup, Erm. Wilco an' out.'

The phone went dead.

'"Wilco an' out"? How does he think 'em up?'

'How does who think what up?'

'Elmer and his stupid "wilco and out".'

'Why did you have to speak to him?'

'"Cos pop and Connor are entertaining the Deputy Sheriff of Fort Jackson together with a couple of Feds. And that kind of suggests the case isn't straightforward.'

'But what reason can there be for that?'

'I wish I knew.'

'Let's go on, shall we?' he gave her arm a reassuring squeeze. 'Perhaps all they're offering is a helping hand.'

She doubted it. But as she chatted on, it didn't take long for her to feel a lot more upbeat. He was a good listener and the chat came easy to him, too. Consequently, it took them no time at all to cover the distance. And, shortly, they were oblivious to anything other than each other. They passed by the inflow of the Big Rock River without comment and only when they reached the grassy area adjoining the lake did they remember to take note of the view. Nat had to admit it was a good one and that he'd hardly noticed it on his previous visit. He stared across the water for a while, his eyes fixed on the jetty opposite.

'One of the problems of being an accountant is...' he spoke softly as if the words were directed more at himself than at his companion. 'is that in one's duties one is often required to detect things, though mainly financial or tax things of course. Nevertheless, at times one may find oneself compelled to use one's ability to detect.'

'Eh?'

'I agree that no one would consider me to be a criminal detective in any shape or form', as he spoke Erm's head moved up and down as if to emphasise the point, 'but to my mind,' he paused to turn and face her again, 'what has been detected so far might be considered to be in the unfortunate state of inconclusiveness and, what's worse, coupled with a strong indication of at least one inherent flaw in the evidence.'

'What the hell are you banging on about?'

He pointed to the jetty on the other side of the lake.

'That's where Warren was shot. Right?'

'Right!'

Nat shook his head. 'Wrong!'

'What d'you mean, wrong?'

'Tell me, Erm, what was the victim doing just before he was shot?'

'According to Annie, he was waving and calling out to her and she was waving and calling back to him when the bullet struck.'

'And whereabouts was she standing?'

'This side of the lake near the other end,' he pushed the penny a fraction further and made it drop. 'You've put your finger on it,' she whooped with glee, 'and no mistake.' Her feeling of elation was such she flung her arms around him. And for once, it wasn't some mature, unattractive female doing the hugging. The experience was one he savoured for as long as he could. In the end, she unclasped him. 'If the shot had been fired at Tate from that end of the lake, it would have hit him sideways on and not straight through the heart. That's assuming the marksman was a good enough shot to hit him with only part of his body showing.'

'And that means,' said Nat, 'that the rifle was fired round about the area where Annie and Bennett were standing.'

'But if that's the case, both Annie and Bennett claimed the sound of the shot came from our end of the lake,' Erm stared blankly at him. 'Also, how did the rifle get from there to here in the first place? It's plain stupid.'

'My thoughts entirely.'

Erm gazed at the density of the undergrowth confronting them. 'But where's the path? If there *is* one - and I somehow doubt there is one on this side of the lake - it sure isn't there now.'

'Perhaps the murderer dropped the rifle off this end by boat?'

Erm pulled a face and shook her head. 'Apart from anything else, a boat would have been in full view of the house and of the jetty on the other side of the lake. And another thing, how did the murderer know where Tate was going to be at the time?' on this, Nat was able to shed some light. 'It's nice to know,' said Erm, with a touch of irony, 'there is some light to be shed on anything to do with this damn case.'

'Although I can tell you why he was where he was, what he was *really* up to is far from clear. Fact is, my client loved to indulge in a spot of fishing on the lake. Not at first light when most devotees would be the stroke of noon. So just before midday each day, he'd pick up his rod and tackle together with a covered basket (presumably to house his catch) and aim for the jetty. He usually opted for the dinghy with the outboard motor. Once aboard, he'd set course for the middle of the lake. And he'd stay put there for about an hour.'

Erm raised her eyebrows in surprise. 'On his own?'

'Always! Though the funny thing is . . .' Nat hesitated, hardly able to credit what he was about to say, '. . . to my personal knowledge, he never succeeded in catching a single fish. I can tell you, if I had to rely on him for my meal each day, by now I'd be nothing but a bag of bones,' Erm stared at his bulk and managed to bite her tongue. 'Though . . .' Nat swung round to face the lake again before going on, 'something's up.'

'You mean, like becoming a bag of bones?'

The words passed over his head whilst he lapsed into silence, that is, until he snapped his fingers and screeched out: 'It's missing!'

'What's missing?'

'The bloody boat!' Nat swung round again. 'Only Warren himself was allowed to put it in place by the jetty ready for use each day. Before I settled down yesterday, I glanced at the jetty. I could swear there was a boat moored between it and the boathouse. So where-the-hell is it now?'

'Was it still there when you woke up?'

'Who knows? I didn't exactly wake up as such. I was rudely brought back to this land of woe and worry by Connor - the raw arm of the law - and bundled off like an old sack of potatoes. At the time, the mooring position of the boat failed to grab my attention.'

'But couldn't it have been put away in the boathouse later?'

Nat was about to challenge her premise, when her mobile buzzed into action.

She grabbed it from the case strapped around her arm. 'Hi, pop,' she said. And that was all she said. From then onwards, hers was a listening role. The Sheriff's instructions were being made crystal clear and she knew by the tone of his voice that he would brook no interruption. The end came abruptly.

'Well?' said Nat.

'No!'

'I take it you decided not to tell your father about our theory as to the position of the gunman when Warren was shot?'

'Pop wouldn't let me get a word in edgeways,' she wrapped her arms around his neck. 'Now brace yourself for the worst,' he did so against her body. And he further extended a hand down on either side of her waist. The worst, he thought to himself? Not from where he was standing. 'Yeah! It's the worst for me. The Feds want to see you, whilst I on the other hand have got to spend my time kicking my heels by the river until the guys from Fort Jackson honour me with their presence and come over and check that damn footprint.'

'Does it mean I'm still a suspect?'

'No, you're not a suspect, Nat. In fact, the Feds seem convinced that you could be their star witness.'

'How-the-blazes can I be a star witness? I was fast asleep at the time. Annie and Bennett are the real star witnesses. It was they who witnessed the murder. And I bet they were the first on the scene, too. Even in normal circumstances, Annie drives her souped-up sports car like a maniac.'

'You've got it wrong, Nat. The chauffeur, Bennett, drove the car.'

'You mean he drove her Mustang?'

'You've got that one wrong as well. He drove Tate's Rolls-Royce.'

'They used *his* Rolls for a picnic?' Nat shook his head repeatedly.

'That's about the size of it.'

'No way! The Rolls was Warren's pride and joy. He'd never allow anyone else to use it.'

'Annie must have applied her extra special charm and kind of persuaded him, don't you think?'

'Come off it, Erm. Annie doesn't even like the Rolls.'

'She's sweet on Bennett, you see, and Tate would insist on him driving it, wouldn't he?'

'Would he? Not for a poxy picnic, he wouldn't, and decidedly not because his niece happens to fancy his chauffeur. It doesn't make sense. Just like it doesn't make sense they think I could have witnessed anything.'

'Its no skin off your nose if the Feds think you did. Neither me nor the Sheriff nor any of his sidekicks is going to argue the toss. If they say black is white, then black *is* white. But it's up to them and not up to us to prove it'

With her hands still draped around his neck and his hands still clasped on either side of her waist, he slid them down until they came to rest on the higher slopes of her lower curves.

She suppressed a giggle.

He suppressed a sigh.

'I can tell you, Erm, Warren's murder is giving me the creeps. I seem to know the answer, but quite frankly it's too absurd to contemplate.'

She told him to zip his lip.

For the second time in twenty-four hours and with the same lush grass beneath his feet, he again felt its natural lure. Sleep, however, was a definite non-starter. And Nat was quick to discover that his fingers were more adept at unfastening the safety pin than they were at fastening it up. On this occasion the synchronisation of his brain's instructions to his fingers as to the movements required to unfasten it was driven on by an irresistible urge...Erm. She was doing the urging.

Chapter Four

Bennett Dwight McCorquodale's feelings were mixed. On the one hand he felt sad at the loss of his employer, but on the other hand he felt he could handle Annie much better than he could handle her predecessor. He expanded his chest and reflected on the quality of his irresistible charm and handsome masculinity. As chauffeur and confidant to the late Warren Tate, it was indeed gratifying to know that Warren's niece, Annie, had taken command (albeit reluctantly) of the situation and at his instigation removed the only influential opposition, Warren's Limey consultant, Nathaniel Foskett.

Apart from acting as chauffeur on behalf of his employer, Bennett undertook the role of Chief Security Officer of the estate. And all the indications suggested that this function would continue under her administration. Admittedly, he'd had to be patient and wait for the appropriate moment when her feelings of grief were less evident, but in the end his strong arm of comfort had done the trick and comforted her into acquiescence. Bennett was convinced Annie would inherit the Fortune Valley estate. On more than one occasion, Warren had hinted as much by describing the main asset bequeathed to her in his will as that which he "treasures most of all ".

Some years ago, Annie's father (Warren's brother) was killed with her mother in a pile-up on the freeway. From then onwards Annie had been living with her great aunt, until her great aunt's death the previous summer, and over the years, she'd transformed Annie into a sophisticated and knowledgeable young lady. As a child Annie was inclined to be squeamish, but by the time she'd reached her teens, the aunt had re-diagnosed the condition and convinced her that she was highly-strung. In addition, the aunt's culinary prowess had been instrumental in transforming Annie's childhood menu of burger and chips to that of *bœuf bourguignon* and *pommes de terre boulangere*. Annie was also aware of the fact that, many moons ago, Warren's estranged wife departed for an undisclosed destination abroad. With no brothers or sisters of her own and no relatives other than Warren himself, there was no doubt in her mind. She *was* his next of kin.

Bennett, too, had been assured of a sizable bequest. At twenty-five years of age, the afro-haired Bennett stood over six feet in his cotton socks and his physique simply rippled with muscles. And he showed them off at each and every opportunity, either on one of his jogs, in the course of patrolling the grounds and gardens of the house, or when swimming in the pool or, as often as not, just stretched out on his back by the side of it. But when night fell, it was a different story. Then he preferred to conduct the function of Chief Security Officer indoors in comfort, in front of a bank of VDUs. Willingly, he allowed his deputy, Craig Deighton, to take over his outside duties. Craig lived locally and at 6 o'clock on the dot each evening he would enter the house ready to protect and detect. On arrival, his first assignment was to make the coffee. Once this had been completed to Bennett's satisfaction, he would check out the garage block and the boat-house. Smartly dressed in uniform and equipped with a gun and a walkie-talkie, he almost matched his boss in stature and air of importance.

By late afternoon the trees were casting long shadows across the lawn. The sound of Oliver Jupp's mower competed with the jabbering chatter of crested jays as they weaved in and out of the trees. With his eyes shielded from the rays of the setting sun by a well-worn cap, Oliver gripped the mower's controls firmly through his protective gloves and directed his efforts to obtaining smooth stripes across the lawn. The birds, on the other hand, directed their efforts abrasively, set perhaps on confrontation. But unlike their human counterparts, they were able to confine their hostilities to mere vocal retorts.

That evening, on his way to the boathouse, Craig's walkie-talkie buzzed into life. He flicked it on nonchalantly.

'Hi, Bennett.'

'Craig! We've got an intruder,' the Chief Security Officer sounded upset. 'I spotted him on the monitor. Came through the side gate bold as brass.'

'D'you mean to say, he let himself in with a key?'

'Guess so.'

'Did you recognise him?'

'Never mind that! Go get him out of here.'

Bennett slammed the receiver down and charged out of the house like a rogue elephant about to do battle.

Craig withdrew the Colt from its holster ready for action. He steamed back to the garage block and in no time at all, espied the outline of a man peering through a window. Craig jerked to a halt and took careful aim.

He called out: 'You're a-trespassing, sonny boy. Stay put and place your hands on the top of your head.'

But Craig was put on the back foot when the man (acting like a rabbit who'd unexpectedly come face to face with a fox) bolted off across a border of shrubs and flowers. Craig gave chase with grim determination. And it didn't take long before Bennett was breathing down his assistant's neck. In the background, Annie's voice was raised and agitated, until it was drowned out by the sound of an over-revved car entering the driveway. The car came to a halt with a screech of brakes.

It heralded the arrival of Mrs Amelia Cadogan, the housekeeper and epicurean cook to the late Warren Tate. Amelia stepped out of the car on to the parking lot at the side of the house, clasping a shopping bag in her elegantly gloved hand. As she did so, her attention was drawn immediately to the chase and to the rabbit facing her in the distance through the trees.

Amelia stood tall and willowy, with dark, tight curls and brown eyes. A widow at the age of forty, she was pleased to think she could still turn a male head or two. She could hear the rabbit panting fit to burst and she could see the fox was almost within pouncing distance.

Up...aim...followed by a precise squeeze.

Cra-a-ack!

Within a split second, the bullet sped from its chamber and struck its target.

The jays flurried from the trees, squawking in confusion and fear. Both rabbit and fox crashed to the ground. Blood dripped down over a clump of white michaelmas daisies, slowly changing their colour into various shades of pink.

Bennett ignored the prostrate Craig and grabbed the rabbit by the collar. He yanked him back up into an upright position.

'You've killed him!' he screeched.

He lifted the rabbit high into the air as if he were no more in weight than a bundle of old clothes. Annie's eyes opened wide in astonishment when she saw that the man being held aloft was none other than Nat.

Racing up from behind, Oliver sped passed her to Craig, who lay spread-eagled across the bed of flowers. Oliver bent over and placed two fingers on the side of his neck. He knelt down and tried his wrist.

No pulse!

In an effort to examine the chest wound, he leaned out further, but after a brief inspection, rose back up on to his feet, shaking his head from side to side.

He turned to Annie.

'I'll call for an ambulance, though I reckon it's too late to do anything.'

He scurried off in the direction of the house.

Annie followed on after him at a slower pace. She was near to tears. The words, poor Craig, filled her mind and caused the tap to drip.

Nat wriggled and wriggled to break loose from Bennett's vice-like grip.

'I didn't do it!' he yelled. 'How could I? You saw what happened. I tripped and fell.'

Bennett's eyes were ablaze.

'How come, Limey, the gun's lying right next to you on the ground?'

Stunned and bewildered, Nat stared down at the gun at his feet. He couldn't offer an explanation. He knew it wasn't his. And it wasn't Craig's either. He could see Craig's gun poking out from under a bush.

With a look of triumph, Bennett fairly chortled at him. 'This time, you ain't gonna get away with it. No sirree! And that's a promise.'

Chapter Five

Sergeant Virgil Schultz of the US Marines instructed his party to "keep close". At the outset, he made them aware that the consequences would be swift and dire should any of them stray from the organised route.

'This,' he advised them, 'is a top security building only open to the public in designated areas.'

That being the case, Virgil spent the duration of the tour with his eyes glued on each and every member of his group. In order to do this, he was required to conduct the entire 75 minute tour walking backwards. His group agreed it was no mean feat and that the tour was both interesting and informative.

The Pentagon is reputed to be the largest building in the world. It stands impressively overlooking the Potomac River at Arlington in Virginia. An exercise in immensity, it houses the US Armed Forces and US Services and Agencies, including the Federal Bureau of Investigation and the Central Intelligence Agency. It contains a maze of corridors (seventeen and half miles of them) and near to 7,800 windows. For a few minutes, Virgil came to a halt to give each of his party the chance to admire the view out of just one of them.

'And as you can see, the interior courtyard is massive and covers an area of five acres.'

They gazed out of it duly impressed.

By coincidence, from the other side of the courtyard another serviceman was looking out of a window. He was wrestling with a potentially explosive situation. In his case the view was of little interest. Neither was aware of the other, nor could they be. The distance between them made that impossible.

General Edwin D. Halstenberg turned away from the window to

face those seated in the room. The group present around the table included the General's aide-de-camp, Major Homer T. Lee, two senior officers (one from the CIA and the other from the FBI), a shared assistant, scribbling away in his notebook, plus Allen 'Buzz' Allenby of the CIA and Spencer Wright of the FBI, both having been urgently recalled from their investigations in Moose City. The sole female present was the CIA agent, Esther Lawrence. The meeting was scheduled as a matter of urgency and the General was the presiding officer.

'D'you mean to say, Buzz,' said the General, worry etched across his well-lined face, 'this guy, Foskett, opened an account at the State Union Bank in Fort Jackson with a banker's cheque for forty thousand dollars and subsequently withdrew half of it in cash?'

'That's correct, sir.'

'Do we know who provided the funds?'

'State Union's giving me chapter and verse. But Foskett can't be all that bright, sir. Apparently, he made no effort to cover it up.'

'I couldn't care less whether he's bright or not. But I do care if it's us and not him who turn out to be the dumb-clucks.'

Buzz eyed him in silence. And that gave Spencer the opportunity to have his say.

'I would advise you, sir, that Foskett used his British passport to open the account. We checked out the number on the passport and the details recorded by one of the bank's managers, a guy called Barton, with the UK authorities and they seemed to add up...that's until he returned yesterday to draw out twenty grand in cash. Unfortunately, he requested and was issued with used bills. But he was again asked to produce his passport as a means of identification. This time, praise be!, acting on our instructions, the teller arranged to have it photocopied before returning it to the customer.'

'And that's when you discovered it was false?'

'No, not exactly, sir. We sent a copy off to the UK and we're still awaiting the result.'

'Correct me if I'm wrong, Spencer, but didn't you say it seemed OK until he returned yesterday?'

'Well, sir,' Spencer's natural caginess was beginning to show, 'the passport disclosed Foskett's age as thirty-eight. The teller was of the opinion the man who withdrew the cash looked younger than that, though it could be he looks young for his age. Also, having seen a copy of the passport, the suspect's photo only vaguely resembles the man I've been tailing for the past half day. But then, most passport photos don't exactly flatter the holder. What clinches it is the fact that I know Foskett wasn't anywhere near Fort Jackson yesterday afternoon. So it doesn't look good, sir.'

'I see,' feeling disgruntled, the General didn't look good either. 'You followed the suspect. OK! Tell us what happened?'

'Not much, I guess.'

'Spencer! Tell us, anyway.'

'Certainly, sir.'

He produced some notes from his pocket and cleared his throat.

'I first picked up Foskett not far from Tate's home when on his way back from the other side of the lake at Fortuna. The Sheriff told me Foskett was over there with one of his officers. Apparently, he was willing to assist the officer in the investigation. He returned on his own, in advance of the officer concerned. For some reason, he deviated on his way back to the highway, where his and the officer's cars were parked, and paid a visit to the boathouse. Afterwards, he returned to his motel. Whilst there, he made one phone call to the Sheriff's office in Moose City. Later, he went back to the Fortuna estate where he spent several minutes giving the cars in and around the garage block the once-over. He was challenged and pursued by the security guard, Deighton. Then the shooting took place and Deighton was shot dead. I witnessed the shooting, so I know Foskett didn't do it, though I'm sorry to say, I didn't see who did.'

'That's a pity,' the touch of sarcasm was lost on Spencer. The General directed his next question at a slim and attractive young brunette seated at the back of the room. 'Esther...you are following this?'

'Indeed I am, sir.'

'So let's get on with it,' the General produced some files from out of a case. 'We're not that concerned should Tate have died as a result of some personal vendetta, but . . .' he raised his fist and smashed it down on the table, 'we would be more than interested should it bear any relationship, however remote, to his activities for and on behalf of us at the Pentagon,' he held up the files to those present. 'These refer to our Gemini trials. The death of one of our agents has cast a shadow over what I believe to be a giant step forward in the war on terrorism. I can tell you the latest trials have been an unequivocal success. In future, we will have the capability to divert any flight to any place at anytime. The pilot and autopilot can continue to control civil aircraft in the air but, if and when necessity dictates, the Gemini autopilot on the ground can, and will, override the aircraft's controls. But should the technical know-how fall into the wrong hands, I shudder to think of the consequences. It could have as devastating an effect as that witnessed on September the eleventh. Due to Tate's capacity to remember everything in microscopic detail, we've made use of his exceptional memory regarding certain sections of the scientific data apropos the creation of Gemini. Tate has been able to move from place to place without us running the risk of losing top secret documents in transit and without attracting undue attention by having to employ personnel to guard such documents. Rest assured, as long as what was inside Tate's brain stayed inside it to the end, our problems are limited. But if it didn't, our problems could be immeasurable. Now has anyone else anything to report?'

'Yes sir!' Buzz spoke out. 'A short while ago, Sheriff Kramer interviewed Foskett. And the upshot is that it's highly likely Tate's murder didn't take place on the jetty as substantiated by the doctor's evidence and the evidence of the two eyewitnesses, Tate's niece, Annie, and the chauffeur, McCorquodale. They were standing a hell of a distance away at the time on the opposite side of the lake. At that distance, the man standing on the jetty need only give the impression of being Tate to be mistaken for him...general appearance, build, clothes and demeanour. I'm sure that would have sufficed. In truth, it's likely the murder took place half an hour or so earlier, at the time when the sound of another shot was heard.'

'Flaming balls of fire! Where does that leave us, Buzz?'

'It leaves us, sir, unable to locate the doctor, Chester Cornell. A vital witness, I would say. He's supposed to be on vacation in the Calghooie National Park, though exactly where, no one knows. We put out an all units call but we've heard nothing as yet.'

'I'm beginning to agree with Spencer. It doesn't look good,' General Halstenberg's furrowed brow creased up even further. 'Buzz...where do you think Foskett fits in to all this?'

'The Sheriff tells us he's been a ready and able assistant. If he was meant to be a patsy, and that is a possibility sir, his natural keenness to find the killer should keep him in a co-operative frame of mind. A definite plus from our point of view, I would say.'

With a nod of the head from the General, directed at his aide-de-camp, the Major produced three sealed envelopes from the bottom of a pile of papers and passed them on to the General.

'As time is the essence, these briefs will specify the direction of your inquiries, covering that which is essential and that which you should leave in the hands of the local or State law enforcement officers,' he leaned over the table and thrust one each under the noses of Buzz and Spencer's superiors. 'Esther,' he called her to his side, 'this one's for you, my dear,' with poise, she rose and glided gracefully towards him. Her lips parted to reveal two rows of perfect whiter-than-white teeth. The smile seemed genuine enough, though Buzz knew otherwise. Her eyes were a dead giveaway, showing hardness and coldness. She retrieved the envelope from the General's extended hand and just as gracefully glided back to her seat. 'You'll liaise with Buzz,' he told her, 'and as you know, he's been operating with Spencer as an FBI agent. You, too, will be undercover, though in a civil capacity as an insurance claims investigator. Major Lee will brief you and let you have the relevant documents. The main thing, Esther, is to make good use of your natural talents...' for a moment he faltered, '. . . err. . .err charm, flair, the art of gentle persuasion, et cetera, et cetera, et cetera. Try and gather as much information as is possible, my dear, from Foskett, Annie Tate, and from the late Warren Tate's staff, not forgetting, of course, the Sheriffs of Moose City and Fort Jackson as well as their respective assistants, especially the one from Moose City who's undertaken most of the groundwork. That's the one Foskett's been assisting and might well prove to be more in the know than either of the Sheriffs in charge.'

Her mouth widened into an arrogant smirk. 'No problem there, sir. In fact, I relish the challenge. I'll endeavour to extract everything worth extracting and I guarantee none of them will feel a thing. And as for the officer who's been with Foskett, I assure you that in no time at all, sir, I'll have him wriggling on the end of my little finger.'

Buzz closed his eyes and in his mind's eye pictured her little finger extended and expanded into the size of a serpent, wrapping itself around some poor, unsuspecting creature and squeezing the very life out of it. As he opened up his eyes again, they were drawn like a magnet to Esther's smug face. His thoughts raced on. Whoever it turns out to be, the poor sod won't stand a chance. It'd take nothing short of a miracle to put one over on Esther.

Chapter Six

Once more Nat found himself the recipient of the Sheriff's hospitality. With hands clasped behind his head, he viewed the interior of his cell from a horizontal position on the bed. Though the cell lacked a radio and television, he thought it could almost be described as homely. But with no drinks on offer (other than a much appreciated supply of coffee) and with food restricted to the culinary capabilities of whichever officer happened to be stuck with the job, Nat concluded that comparisons with the Most Welcome Motel should be restricted to standards of comfort, décor, and facilities of an ablutionary nature. For a while he toyed with the idea of including food, but after consulting Elmer on the subject, he changed his mind. It turned out the dinner served the previous evening was well above average. He studied the primrose painted walls (plain, but in good condition) followed by an examination of the furnishings...a bench seat (a trifle hard on the nether regions, though OK for short sits), plus a table, cupboard and drawers. The sprung bed was as comfortable as one could expect. Also, the cell contained a toilet, shower and hand basin, all discreetly hidden behind a curtain. And they all worked! Without a doubt, he thought, the Sheriff's facilities won by a mile. He concluded that a local criminal's lot was quite a happy one. On the other hand, when contemplating his own particular lot, he looked on it as being not so happy. He'd spent the night in captivity, held, he presumed, on suspicion of murder. No one was willing to tell him anything and, worse still, Erm was noticeable by her absence. His only companion had been a pleasant but inebriated vagrant known as Pie-Eyed Pete, although once a disgruntled Connor had fed him, he seemed to sober up no end. Connor let him have it with the words: "If you try it on again, you'll find an extra pair of balls minced up inside your meatball surprise." Afterwards, Pete was summarily dispatched back into the outside world.

In accordance with the Sheriff's instructions, Connor was acting as chef for the evening. It was a position he considered to be beneath his dignity (and it showed), though to his credit he was a fairly good cook, at least as far as the preparation of fast food was concerned. During the night, Elmer paid further visits to Nat's cell. He turned out to be an affable and willing coffee maker and told Nat they hadn't seen "hide nor hair of the Feds". But funnily enough, he immediately clammed up as soon as Nat asked him why the Sheriff (or anyone else, for that matter) had yet to interview him.

So at sun up, the aroma of coffee once more wafted its way through to him. Within a few minutes a tray and two mugs appeared around the door. This time he was pleased to see the provider was Erm, though he was less pleased to see she came with her chin jutting out in an aggressive manner.

He sat up on the bed and stuck his legs over the side. 'What's the score, Erm?' She glowered at him in silence. 'I didn't kill him, you know,' he assured her. 'I've never fired a gun in my life. Why would I have taken the trouble to phone you yesterday afternoon if I'd intended to do something as diabolical as blowing out the guts of a fellow human being?' Erm's expression eased noticeably.

'Heart.'

'Eh?'

'He was shot through the heart, not the guts.'

'Be that as it may. If I'd carried a gun, why make a dash for it in the first place? In all probability, I could have taken cover round the side of the garage the instant Craig accosted me and fought it out with him, smoky-barrel to smoky-barrel. Though the chances are *I'd* have finished up laid out on the slab instead of Craig.'

'You may be right. But for now I'm more interested in your phone call. Who took the call? No one said you'd phoned.'

She placed the two mugs on the table and propped the tray up against it.

'I left a message with Connor. I said it was urgent and he said you wouldn't be long and he'd let you know on your return.'

'Damn Connor!' She plonked herself down beside Nat on the bed. 'You see, pop was mad at me 'cos you never showed. He reckoned it was my fault. He was as sure as hell I hadn't told you about the Feds wanting to see you.'

'Of course you told me. If only your father had said something. All I was trying to do was to make certain I had a word with you before disclosing my discoveries to the FBI.'

'What discoveries?'

She could see his eyes lighting up at the thought.

'After we parted company yesterday and on my way back to the car, I made a detour via the jetty and boathouse. And guess what I found, or rather, didn't find?' he was too worked up about it to give her time to guess. 'One of the boats is definitely missing, and as far as I know there's only one place on the lake where a boat could be hidden from sight and ideally placed for a getaway.'

Erm knew the exact spot. 'In the bulrushes and reeds at the freeway end of the lake, on the same side as the house.'

'That's the one! The point is why didn't Bennett check the boats? He's in charge of security, isn't he?'

'I'm told he left most of the checking to his assistant, Craig. Maybe that's why he was killed?'

'But if you think that, why am I still under arrest?'

'You're not under arrest, Nat. In fact, you've never been under arrest. Pop could have let you go last night but as we didn't know when the Feds were coming back - and they seemed *real* keen to see you on their return - and as I wasn't too pleased with you, anyway, I thought that it wouldn't do you any harm to hang around a mite longer. Also, I reckoned you would like to be around when the boys from Fort Jackson come up with their findings. They've been checking the gun for dabs whilst ballistics has been checking the bullet dug out of Craig's body. Pop's due to get the results any time now. As for the two Feds, they went on what pop calls "a darn wild goose chase".'

Nat showed no signs of annoyance at being held unnecessarily. Instead, he felt honoured. By his calculations, even at this early stage of their relationship, he felt she considered him to be someone she could readily confide in. As no woman as young and shapely as Erm had ever confided in him before, he decided to find out if her feelings went beyond the scope of the investigation and were more in line with his feelings for her. He began by referring to the inexplicable twists and turns of fate and how one's path in life becomes imperceptibly merged with that of another. She told him to:

'Cut the cackle and get to the point.'

'The point is I haven't a clue as to how highly, or otherwise, you rate me on a personal basis.'

'You aren't fishing for marks out of ten, are you?'

He told her that he rated her ten out of ten and hoped that she would consider participating in a form of celebration he was keen to arrange upon his release from custody.

'What kind of celebration had you in mind?'

'I was thinking more on the lines of a dinner for two.'

Her face lit up as she readily agreed, 'Subject to the formalities being concluded to pop's satisfaction.'

'What formalities?'

'Paperwork to complete. You'll be forced to listen to pop's opinion of Bennett as an eyewitness and of his account as to how Craig was shot. We've enough evidence to suggest he's in urgent need of eyeglasses. There'll be a question or two as well. Like what were you doing prowling around the Fortuna garages? And are your intentions regarding his daughter honourable? That kind of stuff.'

'You are joking, aren't you?'

'No way! The Sheriff's bound to ask what you were doing in the grounds of Fortuna, especially after being told by Annie to sling your hook.'

'I meant about us?'

'Your intentions *are* honourable, aren't they?'

'Of course they are.'

'Then you've got nothing to worry about, have you?' Her eyes twinkled mischievously, though she managed to keep a straight face. 'Now all you have to do, partner, is to explain what you were doing at Fortuna in the first place?' He couldn't believe his ears. She'd accepted his invitation to dinner and was now calling him her partner. She'd said he'd got nothing to worry about. At that moment in time, not a truer word could have been spoken.

'Worry is for those who have something to worry about. What have we got to worry about?' said Nat.

'A murderer on the loose?' replied Erm.

'Apart from that?'

'Me having to wait for an explanation?'

'Point taken! I was checking up on the cars in an effort to discover why Annie used the Rolls in preference to her own car.' Nat observed some doubt in her eyes and in her demeanour. 'I know you think she chose it in order to be alone with Bennett,' Nat continued, 'but she could have been alone with him anywhere in the grounds of the estate. The grounds are big enough for them to get lost in, if they wanted to, and they're big enough for them to have a picnic in, if they wanted to as well.'

Begrudgingly, she admitted there could be something in what he said. But it only added one more imponderable to a mind already filled with imponderables. Try as she may, she couldn't figure out how the murderer could have fired the rifle from the opposite side of the lake (either where Annie was picnicking or somewhere near to where it was found) and also have steered the boat moored by the jetty (the jetty on which the victim was standing when shot) along the bank to the freeway end of the lake. It was nigh impossible. How could the murderer be in two places at once? She put the point to Nat.

He stared blankly at the wall. 'I'm beginning to think that somebody is trying to make a fool of us and up to now has managed to do so with great success. But I have a sneaking suspicion that things are not going according to plan.'

'What makes you think that?'

'The murderer slung the gun at my feet. Doesn't it suggest to you he was trying to implicate me?'

'It sure does.'

'And another thing, where exactly did the FBI men go on their wild goose chase?'

'I don't know where exactly...but something must have happened yesterday afternoon to make them want to get up and go. Whatever it was, it got them both steamed up and on edge. They said it was urgent to have a word with the Doc. You know...he's the doctor who thinks he's in great shape...the flat-chested, fat-bellied, Doctor Chester Cornell,' she let out a derisive snigger. 'According to pop, they're not likely to find him easily for the next two or three weeks. He's on vacation, having fun, if that's the word for it, bird watching; his pet hobby, I guess. Out and about in the Calghooie National Park.'

'Does that mean the Doc was in the house when Warren was shot? For certain, he wasn't there earlier on, prior to the commencement of my initial excursion round the lake.'

'As he was first on the scene, I guess the Doc must have been in the house at the time.'

'And was it Annie who raised the alarm?'

'No! It was Bennett. He phoned the Housekeeper, Amelia Cadogan.'

'So how long did it take for the Sheriff to arrive at the house?'

'He didn't.'

'He didn't what?'

'Arrive at the house.'

'How come?'

'At the time, pop was testing out the extent of his own tender LC on one of his regular monthly visits to his ma in Roseacre, a home for the elderly, built on the edge of the Calghooie National Park. A beaut of a setting and real peaceful like...but a heck of a way from Moose City.'

As she spoke, she leaned across and fingered one of the coffee mugs. It was stone cold.

'I suppose you went in place of the Sheriff.'

'Nope! Pop talked me into tagging along with him.'

'So who went?'

'Connor and Elmer.'

Nat pulled a face. 'Did your father know Warren well?'

'Yeah! Pop used to call on him to go shooting, Wild West style, though it was strictly at a row of tin cans or at a marker on a tree stump...that kind of stuff. Pop's a crack shot, as was Warren Tate. He belonged to pop's gun club in Fort Jackson and the two of them had regular shoot-outs at Fortuna or at the club.'

'And did *you* know Warren well?'

'Nahr! Prancing around like Wyatt Earp isn't my scene. Pop's the only one who had anything to do with him. Together, they reckoned they made a fine pair of rootin'- tootin' cowboys...would you believe? Mom used to call them a couple of Dead-Eyed Dicks. I'm too much of a lady to tell you what I called them.'

'I can't say I blame you. Rootin' tootin' cowboys remind me of my childhood days.'

'Second childhood for some.'

'I didn't exactly help matters by staying on at the motel. I suppose I placed too much reliance on Connor passing on my message.'

She immediately apologised for Connor's failure, but rose to Nat's unintentional bait.

'As soon as I get my hands on him,' she hissed, 'I'll skin him alive.'

'Ah, Erm...' Nat immediately regretted his lack of tact. 'Far be it for me to intervene in such matters or to divert you from your, no doubt, justifiable antagonism, but I would suggest if anyone, it's Bennett, not Connor, who deserves to be skinned alive.'

'You mean, 'cos of what he said?'

'No, not exactly. You see, I still hold a set of keys to the Fortuna house as well as to the access gates around the grounds. If I'd arrived at the garages earlier, I doubt if anyone would have seen me as Bennett wouldn't have been scanning the VDU monitors and Craig wouldn't have arrived for his nightly stint,' he whacked his legs against the side of the bed as if to emphasise the point. 'In the past, I thought I'd got on pretty well with Bennett. But for some unearthly reason, he's changed. I feel as if

I've offended him. Though I don't see how?'

Erm couldn't figure it out either. 'He seems to have it in for you.'

Nat pulled himself up on to his feet and began to shuffle aimlessly about the cell. As he passed by the tray on the floor for the second time, he picked it up and put it on the table.

'Right now, I could do with that cup of coffee we missed out on. It might help me to think straight.'

'Same here,' she patted the bed for him to be seated again. 'If you can wait 'till we see pop, we can get one then.'

'It was just a thought. And right now we're in urgent need of a thought of the inspirational kind.'

'On Bennett, though, don't you reckon it sounds as if somebody may have put the poison in? Maybe that somebody is the murderer.'

'That's an inspirational thought if ever there was one. Bennett must have seen me on the monitors as I entered the grounds and would have recognised me for certain. Now correct me if I'm wrong, but did he instruct Craig to apprehend me as if I were some common or garden trespasser?'

'I guess he did.'

'And did Annie agree with his actions?'

'Far from it. She saw you trip as the shot was fired. She knew you couldn't have pulled the trigger, though she's as mystified as I am as to why you did a runner.'

Her words hit a raw nerve and made him squirm. 'I live in a world of computers, figures, and tax. When faced with a set of accounts, I know what to do and what to expect. But when I found myself staring down the barrel of a gun, the world was alien to me and I'm ashamed to say that my reaction was one of sheer panic. As such, professional accountants rarely panic... though I must admit their clients often do. So I blame myself for Craig's death.'

She wrapped an arm around his shoulders.

'How can *you* be to blame, Nat? The guy who pulled the trigger is to blame ...and no one else. Not even Bennett can be blamed for that.'

'Even so, I can't help thinking that my presence somehow precipitated his death.'

'That's stupid talk! Do yourself a favour and snap out of it.'

Erm's arm was proving to be a great comfort and snapping out of it was getting easier by the minute. And she reckoned it was all in the mind.

'But what's in my mind, Erm, is the fact that the evidence appears to be bereft of logic.'

'You can say that again. It sure don't add up.'

'You sound just like Warren. That was one of his favourite sayings.'

'You mean he was often baffled by something or other?'

'I can assure you there was nothing baffling about him trying to assert his will over a minion like me. To make me feel obligated, Warren would first remind me of something I'd said weeks and weeks ago that may have proved to be a bit off the mark. He would quote me word for word and point out my inadequacies in no uncertain manner. Then he would slip in his usual question. "What do you reckon one and one makes, Nat?" If two happens to be the number that springs to mind, he would have a go at me, and my damn integrity. What he was hankering after was in the form of another question: "What would you like it to make?" You see if the answer was to his liking, he was quite happy to pay the price. And if the "greasing of the palm helps to oil the wheels" - his expression, not mine - I'm certain it must have oiled the wheels on numerous occasions.'

'What are you getting at?'

'What I'm getting at is that people can be bought.'

'True! Some people are willing to give their eye teeth for big bucks, though hardly ever their wisdom teeth.'

'What if there was an arrangement between the murderer and Doctor Cornell? As the facts don't add up, perhaps he's manipulated them in some way? Remember, he *was* first to the body. And don't you think it's rather odd for him to disappear, knowing he's likely to be needed in a murder investigation. And I'll take a bet the FBI won't have much luck in finding him, either. So bearing that in mind, what about us going through the so called facts together to see if we can spot what is fact and what is fiction?'

'I agree!'

And Erm was about to put forward her ideas on the subject when an unusually affable Connor strode into the cell.

'The Sheriff would like to see you both,' he informed them, 'and ballistics has confirmed that the gun found by Nat's feet *is* the murder weapon. No luck with dabs though. The killer must have worn gloves.'

Erm's response was to rise from her seat on the bed and turn on Connor hissing like a cobra. But instead of a snake's venomous forked tongue, she extended two of her fingers to within an inch of his solar plexus.

'Just the guy I wanted to see. Tell me, Connor, when d'you think you're going to get around to letting me know about the phone call Nat made yesterday?' Her words together with the extended fingers wiped the smile off his face in a flash.

'I was fair rushed off my feet at the time, Erm. It got pushed right out of me mind. Hell's bells, I only came in here to pass on a message.'

'Like what you didn't do yesterday.'

'I'm real sorry.'

He looked it, too, and with his eyes riveted on the fingers about to be dug into him, his sorrow was centred more on his own precarious position than on his failure to inform Erm.

'Do you happen to know if any gloves were found?' Nat asked Connor.

'Is it OK for me to answer him, Erm?'

'See if you can answer the question well enough for me to think that you're on the ball this time.' She raised the hand with the fingers extended and wagged them under his nose. It had the effect of easing him out. Two fingers in the air were no longer such a threat.

'Oswald got us to do a recce of the area, but we couldn't find any gloves as such.'

'As such?'

'I mean to say, Nat, not what you call a proper pair of gloves.'

'What don't you call a proper pair of gloves?'

'For starters, the ones I found weren't in good condition. They were gardening gloves, all torn and holed. I found 'em stuck inside one of the bushes. The gardening guy, Oliver, told Oswald it happened way back. Said all the holes used to rile him some and one day he got so fed up with 'em, he slung 'em away. Later, when he tried to find 'em to bin 'em properly, he couldn't.'

On hearing this, Nat looked at Erm knowingly.

'You don't realise, Connor,' said Erm, raising but a solitary finger at him this time, 'that the only reason you're the acting Deputy Sheriff is that pop has been told by some creep in authority that it's *man's* work. Pop resents it. I resent it. If you ever give me half a chance again, you'll resent it, too, doubled up before you or anyone else can say "sexist".'

'Rules are rules. Surely the message weren't that important?'

'Let me tell you, Connor,' she glowered, 'Nat checked it out and there's a boat missing. Guess who's going to volunteer to locate it?'

'But I've been on duty all night.'

'Shut-eye or no shut-eye, you owe me one.'

At which, Connor resigned himself to the inevitable.

Chapter Seven

Moose City is a misnomer. In living memory no one has ever seen or heard of a moose in its vicinity. And as for it being a city, the accuracy of the description is questionable. It is neither large nor is it thriving. Perhaps at best, one could say it jogs along at a constant rate. It's said that the word "moose" originated through the misspelling of the name of a local Indian Chief, Wapetee. He resided in the region in the 1840s, not long after the first settlers arrived. In those days, the area around the Big Rock River was referred to as Wapetee County. In the course of time and after the establishment of a trading post and a Bearded Order of Monks farming high above on the Big Rock Ridge (on the present-day site of the Saint Luke's Monastery), the name Wapetee became Wapiti. As wapiti is the name for an American variety of moose, when the trading post eventually expanded into a town, the town became known as Moose and ultimately, Moose City.

　　　Whatever the reasons may have been for its origination, the visitors to Moose City invariably find it a most agreeable place. The street, Main Boulevard, with its broad avenue of trees and wide pavements, runs from the highway to the shopping precinct on its way to various public buildings. It skirts the Municipal Offices (including the Sheriff's office) and finishes up at the town's City Park. Linked together by a pedestrian bridge, the park extends to either side of the Big Rock River and contains eye-catching displays of Californian godetias (rose-red, white, and crimson) set here and there in various shapes carved out of the grass. The multicoloured South African geraniums also catch the eye, as do the aristocrats of the buttercup family, the grand peony. It's a place for the visitor to walk or jog, or just to sit and rest and to spend time around the bandstand, listening to the band, or around a small man-made lake, or in one of the lake's hides studying a variety of bird life. All within wrought-iron gates and old stone walls.

Among the visitors taking the air in the park this particular afternoon was a very contented soul. He could see a light at the end of the tunnel, even though in Erm's opinion the light was not much more than a flicker and its brightness could still do with a boost. But the really important thing was to be back in Annie's good books and back as a guest in the Fortuna residence, once more experiencing the joys of civilised living, including Amelia Cadogan's epicurean delights and away forever, he hoped, from the unpalatable fast food and the discomforts of the most unwelcome Most Welcome Motel. Even more satisfying was Erm's acceptance of his invitation to spend an evening out together.

As Nathaniel Foskett ambled along, things seemed to be on the up

'Hi Nat!'

The voice of greeting came from Hank Kepler, the proprietor of Hankering, a local store providing useful and unusual knick-knacks, exotic sweetmeats and quality wines. Nat recognised the voice instantly.

'Are you by any chance,' Nat chirped, 'heading for your store? If so, I'd like to pop in later for a bottle of your best château burgundy. A gift for Annie.'

'You old romantic!' as he spoke, Hank's small, round spectacles bobbed up and down precariously on the end of his nose. His craggy features split into a smile. 'Don't you mean, your little amoroso?'

'No, I don't!' Hank's insinuation flustered him into a forceful denial. 'If you must know, it's purely a thank-you gift for Annie now that I've returned to the fold at Fortuna Valley.'

Hank Kepler gave him a sly wink. 'I'll believe you, though

thousands wouldn't. Give me twenty minutes or so . . .' he pointed to a group of monks, seemingly huddled together in prayer. '. . . as I must sort this bunch out first.'

Nat's initial glare melted into a blank stare.

'You help them spiritually?'

Hank clasped his sides and let rip a roar of laughter.

'They're not praying, Nat, but trying to listen into the latter part of the commentary on the local ball game, you know, our great American religion... baseball! The Moose Elks are in the local final against those Jackson jerks and we aim to pulverise 'em, and as far as I can tell, that's what we're doing,' he waved his hand in the general direction of the monks. 'Trouble is, their radio's on the blink. As likely as not it's in need of a new battery, but they always kick up a hell of a fuss when it comes to whose turn it is to fork out for a new one. You can see how they're having to lean over in a circle to hear anything,' Nat's blank stare turned into a look of astonishment as he watched Hank gain attention by patting the raised posterior of one of the participants. 'May I join you, Brother Constantine?' he asked, as he bent his lanky frame and stuck his head into a sea of hair and whiskers. He was welcomed by a mixture of hellos and shushes. 'Now your trip's been delayed,' he whispered loudly, 'I'd better give all of you the once-over in the morning. I wouldn't want any of you to let the side down, and in return, a glass or two of your excellent applejack will be reward enough.'

Nat let loose his parting shot.

'After you've finished base-balling about, Hank, I'll see you later on at Hankering for that bottle of wine.'

But Hank was in no position to respond. To gather the gist of even a part of the intermittent commentary capable of being heard necessitated a concentration level of 100 per cent, although for a few moments his mind wandered as he toyed with the idea of donating a new battery himself.

As Nat moved off, he noticed another monk standing alone by the side of the path in the shadow of the trees. He couldn't help but wonder why he hadn't joined in with the others. Also, he pondered over the name of the opposing team, the Jackson Jerks. It sounded derogatory to say the least but as his knowledge of baseball was next to nothing, they could have started out as a team of weightlifters for all he knew.

With Hank's nose pointing downwards, Nat also pondered over the likelihood of his spectacles finishing up smashed to bits around his feet. Somehow, though, they never seemed to fall off even when the pull of gravity suggested they should. He deliberated on the matter for a time and came to the conclusion that the tip of Hank's upturned nose must either contain magnetic-like properties or be smeared with a substance similar in effect to that of Velcro. As he approached a bend in the path, he mulled over Hank's predication as to the inevitability of the outcome. Nat was certain they'd celebrate it vociferously.

With arms raised aloft, Hank and his merry band of monks cheered the final victory. But it was during a lengthy discussion on the merits of each member of the team that Hank happened to glance down at his wristwatch and was quick to realise that from his wife, Minnie's, point of view, he'd overstayed his welcome. With a call of "see you", he took leave of the men of the cloth and made rapid tracks to the other side of the park and on to the store, Hankering, at the end of the shopping precinct.

Due to the Elk's success, he was still on cloud nine as he passed through the entrance to the store. But once inside, his euphoria was blasted out of all existence by the force of his wife's tongue.

'Where the hell have you been?'

He staggered back against the door.

'I. . . I met the Brit, Minnie. You know...that guy, Nat. We had a bit of a powwow. He's real interesting, honey. Guess I forgot the time.'

Wilhelmina Kepler crossed her arms over her Double-D bust and stuck out her chin. Her ample girth moved to and fro menacingly. 'Oh,yeah! Pull the other,' with a shrug of her shoulders, she brushed her husband's suggestion aside.

He began to quiver, as did the glasses on the end of his nose. 'But, Minnie, honey, you're always saying we must put the customer first. Nat's a good customer, isn't he? Said he'd drop in for some vintage wine,' Hank waited to see if he'd already done so. She made no comment. He heaved a sigh of relief. 'You speak to him, honey. He'll confirm it for sure.'

'No point! If that's who you're telling me you saw...guess that's who you saw. But you sure ain't telling me what you an' the Limey got up to, are you?' she turned away in disgust. 'Knowing you, you'll have arranged with him to cook up the usual crop of lies and weak excuses,' she aimed her bulk towards the room at the back of the store. 'As it happens, ma's been keeping me company, so if you'll excuse me, and by the by, I'd like to remind you that's the only kind of excuse I ever have to give you, I'll rejoin her, whilst you start to do what you were supposed to do earlier on...check out what stock needs replacing or marking down.'

Hank shuffled his feet awkwardly.

'Yeah, Minnie...will do.'

As he spoke, the mother's diminutive figure appeared in the room's doorway. Remarkably, she was unlike her daughter both in appearance and disposition. Always sympathetic and understanding, she held a soft spot for her son-in-law.

'Hi-yer, Hank!' she called out. 'As the customers are sparse at the moment, if I were you, I'd bolt the door. It'll give you a bit of peace and quiet whilst you're working. And anyone needing to come in, urgent-like, can knock. Also,' she winked, 'soon as you give me the nod, I'll put the percolator on.'

'Thanks, ma.'

He returned her wink with an appreciative grin.

As recommended, he bolted the door and moved the sign to CLOSED. He spent some time pinpointing the position of the stock in question and once he'd rolled up his sleeves, he was ready to hump the discountable items to their allotted shelf. From the backroom the two women could hear the sound of his exertions as he huffed and puffed away.

In a short while, mother and daughter were absorbed in all the local gossip, though they did pause in their deliberations for a moment when the door's buzzer sounded followed by a murmur of voices.

With deftness, the visitor stepped behind Hank and wrapped an arm around his neck. The pressure applied to his throat prevented him from crying out. Hank grabbed the offending arm and tried to pull it away. As his efforts became more and more frantic, his nails dug deep enough to produce streaks of blood beneath the assailant's clothing. The grip tightened and tightened until sufficient leverage was obtained to yank him off his feet. For once, Hank's glasses no longer defied the pull of gravity and skidded across the floor with hardly a sound. He kicked out in every direction, including in the direction of one of the display stands. But the crash that followed did no more than raise an eyebrow and a comment from Minnie as to her husband's 'ham-fisted ways'.

Back in the store, Hank's eyes were bulging out of their sockets. His tongue lolled out like a panting dog, but bereft of the sound of its pant. The crack that followed was loud enough to be heard in the other room. As it was, the women's ears were deaf to anything other than their own voices. Swiftly and silently Hank was laid out on the floor behind the counter. For a second time, the door's bolt was withdrawn and the buzzer sounded as the visitor departed at pace into the street beyond.

Earlier on in the park, en route for Hankering, Nat was rounding the bend in the path when who should he bump into but the provocative and shapely figure of officer Ermentrude Kramer in the course of undertaking her park patrol duties on the beat.

Nat was baffled. 'How on earth could something like park patrol take precedence over a murder investigation?'

Erm was quick to explain.

Apparently, the FBI assisted by Fort Jackson's Sheriff and Deputy had taken charge of the case. If need be, Moose City police can assist...but only if need be. Erm felt so incensed by the decision, she opted for park patrol. As it was generally quiet and uneventful, she thought it might give her time to ease herself out. In reality, the opposite proved to be the case. She'd spent most of her time chewing over what she considered to be a damn insult.

Meeting her partner in the investigation was a great help as she was able to pour her heart out to him to such an extent, Nat readily agreed with her suggestion for them "to carry on with the good work, whether those stuck-up sods like it or not". She invited Nat to accompany her on her way back to the Sheriff's office. As Hank's store was situated between them and the office, it seemed to fit in well with their respective itineraries and, as far as she was able, she filled him in on the current developments in the case.

Connor had come up trumps! He'd located the missing boat. It was well concealed, but positioned more or less as they'd predicted. Also, he'd spotted a couple of footprints on the bank as well as some tyre marks near the road. This indicated the place where a getaway car was parked.

As usual, the boys from Fort Jackson were dealing with it, but as pop insisted on being kept in the picture, they would fill him in...eventually.

As yet, they'd had no luck in identifying the other footprints discovered by Nat when on their lakeside jaunt together. The tread and size of the shoe had been checked against a variety of men's footwear covering both the Fortuna residents and known visitors, but no match was found.

'And another thing, Nat,' Erm continued, 'it seems some guy kidded a bank in Fort Jackson into opening up an account in your name. He did it with a banker's cheque . . . guaranteed good no matter what. Pop was told it referred to a "Letter of Credit" issued by a bank in Washington DC.'

Nat could hardly contain himself. 'You mean to say someone's deliberately tried to put me in the shi . . . mire?'

"fraid so. Buzz told pop but didn't say who it was,' she shrugged her shoulders. 'Though lucky for you, he did say you're in the clear.'

Nat blew his top.

'Lucky for *me*?' he shrieked. 'Who the hell is Buzz?'

'Calm down, will you? He's one of the Feds.'

'And did this "one of the Feds" reveal who authorised the Letter of Credit?'

'Not to pop he didn't.'

'It strikes me this Buzz chap is not the communicative sort.'

'Maybe he doesn't know the answer?'

'You must be joking! The cheque will show the bank it's drawn on and the Letter of Credit can be traced back to the originator. That means Buzz should know the identity of the person who provided the funds. Under the circumstances, why don't we put him in his place.'

'And how do we do that?'

He gave her a sly grin.

'Remember? My discoveries not only covered the missing boat but what I believe to be the true reason why Annie made use of the Rolls at the time. Didn't you tell me that the FBI are convinced that the man on the jetty wasn't Warren but some look-alike?'

'According to pop, that's what they reckoned. But what are you driving at?'

'What I'm driving at is why don't we give this Buzz person something to really think about? Let him see what a lousy detective he is.'

'I agree he's lousy, but as to being a lousy detective..?'

'That's providing Annie did what I think she did.'

'And if she didn't?'

'I know Annie and how she would react where her one and only uncle was concerned. Let me explain,. . . '

She listened to him attentively and without comment until he'd finished. She hoped he was right. Inwardly, he hoped so too. He suggested she should accompany him on his visit to Annie once he'd picked up the bottle of burgundy from Hank.

'And perhaps later, we could focus our minds on our evening out together. I can recommend a particularly good restaurant in Fort Jackson. French cuisine at its very best.'

'Sounds great,' though her voice sounded flat. 'Don't you think the main thing is for us to enjoy a meal together?'

'Absolutely! I'm all for it.'

'I'm glad you agree.' The look she gave him was one of relief.

'Meanwhile, once you've spoken to Annie, I'm convinced it will get you a well deserved pat on the back.'

'But it *is* your idea,' said Erm

'But you're the one who's going to put it over.'

'Thinking on, though, you're due for something a damn sight better than just a pat on the back . . .' She stifled a giggle. '. . .that's if you play your cards right.'

'I tend to lose at cards,' said Nat

'They say..."unlucky at cards, lucky in love".'

'I've always been unlucky at cards and the lucky in love part has taken a hell of a time in coming.'

'But it sure is coming,' she let out a less stifled giggle.

He heaved a deep sigh. 'I thought you meant . . .?'

'Look!' she pointed at Hank's store as it came into view round a bend. 'We'll be there in a couple of minutes.'

'I thought you meant . . .?'

She jerked him to a halt square on. 'Don't think! Just listen carefully to my prophecy as I study your phizog,' she gazed into his eyes. 'I can see a new romance about to hit you. A sexy brunette is craving for your company. One who would love to (her words, not mine) meet up with you at a time and place convenient to yourself. Could it be at your place or hers? Your eyeballs are too red for me to see.'

'My eyeballs aren't red, Erm.'

'Give it time. I can see her desires going far beyond the body stage. You must ask yourself, will I be able to satisfy her every need? Bearing in mind she could be a mite too hot for you to handle. I'm sure she lusts for something. Can you think what it is?'

'I dread to think.'

'She lusts for in-for-mation. And her name is as sweet as she is, Esther... Esther Lawrence. And she's in to all kinds of things, including insurance. I can tell you she has a sylphlike figure, she's polite without meaning it, and damn good-looking too. In fact, she's the kind of girl I can't stand the sight of...and vice versa, I'm glad to say.'

With a chuckle, they continued on their way.

'What sort of insurance are we talking about?'

'She assesses claims, and she's nosey with it, too. Wants to know who's going to cop what in the Tate estate, 'specially the proceeds of his life policies. Seems to think you'll have all the answers, you lucky so-and-so.'

'Lucky? You're both round the twist, and speaking of round the twist, let's brace ourselves for Hank.'

'Still, life would be dull without a couple of oddballs here and there.'

'You have to admit, there's nothing wrong with my...'

'No need to paint a picture.'

'my sense of humour over a leg-pull,' joked Nat.

She giggled.

He grinned back at her as he pushed open Hankering's door and waved her in.

'And,' he added, as he followed on into the store, 'if Hank so much as makes the slightest suggestive remark about us two arriving together, so help me, I'll break his ruddy neck.'

Chapter Eight

Annie Tate moved restlessly on the settee as she stared into the expressionless face of the grey-bearded lawyer sitting beside her.

'As well as a relative, Warren was a very special friend. And I do appreciate you coming to see me, Max, but...' she brushed away a tear, 'if at all possible, I'd rather not have to consider money matters at a time like this.'

'I can assure you, Annie, who gets what is not up for discussion,' Max Goldbloom puffed away at his cigar. 'All I am aiming to do is to make sure you understand the ins and outs. As executor, the will directs me to distribute the assets and to initially administer and maintain the estate on behalf of the residuary legatee.'

'That's the main thingy, isn't it?'

'If you mean by that the one who's due to inherit the bulk of the estate, yes, she is,' Annie gave him a knowing look, 'and as I've already explained, I'm not permitted to divulge the contents of the will until after the funeral.'

'That's something I'd rather not think about.'

'The will?'

'No...the funeral.'

'Good grief, Annie. That's life! Here today and...'

'Gone and forgotten, that's what I reckon, young lady.' Rosie Witherspoon, Amelia Cadogan's culinary assistant and the house's general dogsbody, cut short the lawyer as she entered the room.

'Who's gone and forgotten?'

'The Limey, Annie! He hasn't turned up.'

'He's been delayed,' said Annie.

'And you forgot to tell me, did you?'

'I don't have to tell you everything.'

'As I'm the one who lets 'em in, I'm the one to tell. Otherwise, I tell 'em to get lost. Matter of fact, I've got Miss Esther Lawrence outside champing at the bit, wanting to see you as well as the missing Limey.'

The interruption gave the lawyer the excuse to leave he was waiting for. He made for the door with his cigar stuck in the air in the form of a farewell salute.

'Warren will be moved from the morgue to the Chapel of Rest the day before the you know what. Should you care to look in on him, they'll leave the lid off. If not, they'll screw it down.'

Annie made it clear she favoured the latter.

'All being well, I'll see you at the you know what.' A trail of ash plotted his route across the carpet.

Annie was well aware of Rosie's capacity to stir things up, either in the kitchen, whilst producing something on Amelia's behalf, or with her big mouth. Unattached, mid-forties, short, and with straight, mousy hair, her round, bluish-grey eyes matched an equally round face. As far as Annie was concerned, she exuded a kind of possessive maternal instinct with plenty of lip.

'Will you please show her in, Rosie.'

She leaned over Annie seated on the settee and whispered in her ear: 'I tell you, young lady, this one's a hard cow.'

Annie was about to administer a rebuke when Rosie spun round and charged back through the open door. She closed it behind her and raised her voice.

'Miss Tate will be pleased to see you, Miss Lawrence. And although we think she's in line to cop the lot, she's feeling a mite too fragile to talk about it right now, though I'm sure she'll do her best to answer all your questions, providing you do your best to cut out the usual flimflam.'

Esther gave Rosie a withering glance. Rosie, for her part, beamed back at her before heading for the kitchen. It seemed to put Esther on the back foot. From inside the room, Annie glared at the door. It didn't take much for her to work out that Rosie had been eavesdropping.

To ensure she looked calm and focused, Esther delayed her entry into the room. She pulled her lips back and pushed her whiter than white teeth forward. Once set and in control again, she strode on through the doorway with one hand on her briefcase and the other hand outstretched invitingly.

'I'm dee-lighted to meet you, Miss Tate...Annie.'

After going through the motions of shaking hands, Annie directed her guest to an easy chair opposite the settee. Esther slid into it, opened up her case, and produced from it a wad of papers. She spent some time sifting through them before placing a couple significantly on her lap. She returned the others to the case, resting it on the arm of her chair.

'As a representative of Amalgamated Life Corporation, my job is to investigate, to verify, and ultimately to advise my clients as to their pecuniary liabilities in respect of the two policies previously entered into by Warren Tate with my clients for the sum of...' she paused and held up the papers on her lap, 'a quarter of a million dollars each. And in order for me to assess the claim, I need as much background information as possible leading up to Warren Tate's tragic death.'

As Annie's answers were based on guesswork, Esther (and her smile) suffered a setback. And once she discovered Annie was unaware of the contents of the will, what was left of her smile vanished altogether. Esther felt in need of a stiff drink, but kept her mouth shut when all Annie offered her was a cup of coffee.

It took three pushes of the intercom button and a long wait before Rosie decided to respond.

Yes...she had heard the button. Yes...she had been keen to answer. But it just so happens her cake had reached a tricky stage in its preparation and what with Amelia being out on one of her shopaholic sprees, she felt duty bound to keep at it, as instructed. Surely, no one could fault her for that, could they?

They were pleased to hear that the coffee together with some savoury titbits would be on their way before either of them could say "sweating-buckets-working-fingers-to-the-bone".

Neither of them was inclined to put it to the test.

Whilst they were waiting, Esther inquired as to Nat's present whereabouts. Although he'd been due to call, Annie was advised of a delay. Apparently, he was giving Oswald and Erm a helping hand in the investigation and would be along as soon as he was free. Erm would be accompanying him in order for Annie to clarify the position relating to an area of concern in the investigation. Just prior to her visit, Esther had been advised of the latest fatality but no mention was made of Nat's presence. She mulled over as to what the circumstances or piece of evidence could be within the area of concern? With bitterness, Esther recalled her interview with Erm and how the minimum amount of information took the maximum amount of effort in continual probing. Her frustration bubbled up inside her as she realised that Erm had kept her in the dark and it fully occupied her thoughts until the chink of cups heralded the arrival of the coffee.

Rosie placed the tray on the coffee table and was about to pour out when Annie noticed that the tray contained two extra cups.

'Have we company?' she inquired.

'Didn't I say?' came the reply. 'I've just let the Limey in with his po-lice escort. At present, they're making use of the johns.'

As she spoke, Erm and Nat entered the room.

Annie effected the introductions, though none were needed in the case of Erm and Esther. It seemed they'd both met before and were now "true-blue buddies". Just to prove the point, each landed a peck on the other's cheek.

The new arrivals were seated on the settee, either side of Annie. They thanked Rosie for the coffee and savoury titbits as she passed them around.

'If any of you wants anything more or wants a top-up of coffee...no sweat! All you need to do is buzz. I'll be in the kitchen, up to me eyeballs in it, as usual.'

Rosie withdrew sporting a grin of immense proportions. Annie moved her lips, but 'thanks' stuck hard in the throat.

As he called out her name, Annie turned her head to face Nat.

'I owe you an apology,' he said, 'and I do hope you'll forgive me.'

'There's nothing to forgive.'

'Yes, there is. I've failed to bring you my intended "thank you for letting me stay" gift. It was going to be a bottle of Hank's best burgundy.'

'I'm sure you had your reasons.'

'Regretfully, I did. Hank's been murdered.'

Annie let out a wail and buried her head in his chest. Nat's arms hovered about in space behind her back.

'Did you know Hank well, Annie?' Erm inquired with some concern.

'No-o-o! Hardly at all.'

'She takes everything to heart, does our Annie.' Nat's hands came to rest on her shoulders. 'But she must try and buck up soon. Erm has a question in urgent need of an answer, and one thing's for certain, we do want to find the murderer, don't we?'

Annie sat up straight again and proceeded to dab her eyes with a tissue.

'Do you think, Erm, it's the same person who killed Warren?'

'It could be, but if it isn't, we feel sure the murders are connected in some way.'

'Before you put your question to Annie,' said Nat, 'may I first pose a question or two of my own to Miss Lawrence?'

Erm said, 'OK', and Esther's OK came in the form of show of teeth.

'Please call me Esther,' she cooed at him, 'as Miss Lawrence sounds much too formal, don't you think?'

'Sorry, Esther,' though he didn't look it, 'I believe you assess insurance claims? If so, may I ask on whose behalf?'

'On behalf of Amalgamated Life Corporation, Nat. I'm attempting to assess the potential claims arising on Warren Tate's death. I hold details relating to two current life policies.'

'Current? Do you mean, they were recently taken out?'

'Oh, no...they were taken out years ago.'

'I see! That really is most helpful.'

He leaned forward to address Erm. 'The floor's all yours.'

She stared back at him quizzically. She didn't understand the reason for his questions nor the significance of Esther's answers. But she knew by his expression they must be of importance.

She turned her attention to Annie.

'I hope my question won't upset you any further, but we do need to know that on the day Warren died, it was truly, truly him you saw standing on the jetty on the other side of the lake, bearing in mind you and Bennett were a fair distance away from him at the time?'

'I've already answered that one.' The question didn't so much upset her as irritate her. 'I told the Sheriff. I told the FBI men. I told Connor. I even told Elmer. Now it seems, you need to be told as well. Listen carefully, Erm, and if you're still uncertain, please have a word with all the others. *It was Warren!*'

'But at that distance, how can you be so sure?'

'Easy! Warren always kept a pair of binoculars in the Rolls. Bennett and I trained them on the jetty and we saw him as large as life,' she squirmed at her own description, 'I mean...we saw him for sure.'

Esther glanced down at her watch and nervously fiddled with the strap. 'I'm sorry I can't stay any longer. I'm running late for my next appointment.' Erm rose with the others to bid her goodbye. She registered a peck on Esther's cheek. Esther reciprocated, and Annie followed suit. Nat declined. He offered a hand instead.

'We must go, too, Erm,' said Nat, 'to discuss matters with your father, et cetera.'

'And between ourselves?'

'That too.'

The four walked towards the side door and as Annie opened it, she was confronted by the sprightly figure of a ruddy-faced Oliver Jupp.

'Come and have a look, Annie,' he said invitingly. 'I've dug out that old shrub overhanging the steps. You were going to consider how best to fill the gap.'

'I'll be with you in a jiff, just as soon as I've seen off my guests.'

Oliver eyed them up and down with interest before withdrawing to where he'd left his gardening tools and implements straggling the steps leading to the driveway.

Whilst Erm and Nat were engaged in giving Annie a goodbye embrace, Esther descended the steps at pace and hurried across to her car.

With hardly a glance in their direction, she drove off at speed.

'Remember, Nat,' Annie called out after him as he and Erm followed on down the steps, 'it's fillet steak en croûte for dinner tonight with your favourite sweet to follow...crème brulee.'

'Sorry, Annie, I'll have to be excused this time. I'd love to indulge in one of Amelia's specialities but Erm and I hope to be sampling something somewhat similar ourselves this evening in Fort Jackson.'

'Good for you...and for you, too, Erm,' she waved to them from the top of the steps. 'Have a great time,' she shouted.

They returned her wave. And as they started to walk across the driveway, Nat instinctively held Erm back. He could hear the distant sound of a revved-up engine. This was followed by a blast of a horn and a screech of brakes. He knew that Amelia Cadogan was in the driving seat. She greeted them with an elegantly gloved hand thrust up through the open sunroof.

They continued on to Erm's patrol car. She took the wheel but didn't turn the key.

'Well?' she said, with an air of impatience.

'Not well for Esther.'

'Who cares about her?'

'But isn't she supposed to be your new true-blue buddy?'

'Never mind that. Tell me what you think?'

'I think some of the facts are suspect.'

'Yeah! And we both reckon the doctor's to blame.'

'And then there's the ballistics report.'

'How can that be suspect?'

'Not suspect as such. Just misconstrued.'

'How?'

'I'll explain later.'

'And another thing . . .'

'Let's go, Erm!'

'Apart from pop, who else is included in your et cetera?'

'Only Connor.'

'Why do we need to see him?'

'You're keeping Annie waiting.'

Erm started up the engine and pressed the accelerator. They gave Annie a final wave as they passed her on the steps, but before the car reached the outer gates, Erm opened up again.

'Annie's no longer waiting. But I am.'

'Where shall I start?'

'Esther, ballistics, or Connor? You choose.'

'Esther's a fraud. Warren didn't have any life cover.'

'You reckon she's not acting for Amalgamated Life?'

'Oh, she's acting all right, and pretty convincingly for the most part, but not for a life company. Though for whom, who can say? As for Connor, he was there with Elmer and undertook the initial investigation not long after Annie and Bennett witnessed the shooting.'

'So what?'

'So only Connor and Elmer can answer questions directly relating to it. The point is, partner, I suspect who our murderer is, but if I tell you who I suspect, you'll think I've gone stark raving bonkers.'

'Why on earth should I think that?' he whispered the name in her ear. For a moment, the car swerved out of control. 'You're mad! You almost made me crash.'

'It's the only thing that makes sense.'

She swallowed hard. 'I refuse to comment until you've tested your theory out on pop. Just remember, he doesn't suffer fools gladly. Not that I'm saying you *are* one. Chances are, I could be one for doubting you.

Meantime, shall we consider ballistics?'

'The science of projectiles. Tell me, what does it prove?'

'That the bullet extracted from the body came from a specific weapon.'

'And that's all.'

'But if you're right, and I repeat, *if* you are, your point about the ballistics report would be valid. Even more so, if we take into account where the murder weapon was found, near to where you were snoring your head off.'

'I can assure you, Erm, I was not snoring my head off. I never snore my head off.'

'Connor said it was loud.'

'You can't go on what he says.'

'In that case, why d'you want to see him?'

Nat glared at her. 'Let's concentrate on another anomaly, shall we?'

'Such as?'

'When we left, did you notice how clean the gardener's shoes were?'

'I guess you've really flipped this time.'

'As he said he'd been digging, don't you think his shoes should have been at least just a teensy-weensy bit soiled?'

'Maybe he changed them beforehand.'

Nat doubted it.

As they arrived at the parking lot behind the Sheriff's office, Erm snapped her fingers in annoyance.

'What am I thinking of? Pop will be home by now.'

'No problem, Erm. We can see him there, if you like.'

'What a great idea! We can sort out Connor first as he'll still be inside. Afterwards, we can be on our way to pop and mom. I know we were due to go out tonight, and I don't want to disappoint, but...' she could hardly contain herself. 'Don't you think it's about time you tried some good American cooking for a change instead of that pretty-pretty French stuff? All display and no guts. We can always go out another night, can't we? And you did say togetherness was the main thing. And we would be together, wouldn't we?' she didn't wait for a reply. 'If it's OK with you, and I shan't mind a bit if it isn't...' Nat smiled in acquiescence. He knew instinctively she could well mind a lot. 'Why don't you stay on for dinner? Mom's been dying to meet you. She's doing her Hamburger Special tonight. You'll love it! Charred to purr-fection...smoky crispness around the edges but with the juiciest of centres. Jacket potatoes, sour cream and chives, all topped with mom's favourite ketchup, and you can't beat her Blueberry Pie,' a fillet steak en croute and a crème brulee flashed before his eyes, 'and to wet your gullet a treat, you can't beat good old Uncle Sam's beer either. Or if you prefer it, you can join pop in a finger or two of rye instead? Or why not try pop's wine? He gets it by the boxful.'

'The *boxful*?'

'Cool, eh? It's the in-thing. Pop always says "Dan's Liquor Centre for the Discerning Drinker" is best. They're the cheapest in town and they deliver to your door, too, providing you buy a dozen or more boxes at a time. And it's real good stuff made from genuine grapes crushed under foot. It says so on the box.'

A bottle of vintage claret flashed before his eyes. With a pronounced droop of the shoulders, he croaked: 'Sounds great to me, Erm.'

Having bought it locally, Nat clasped in his hand a large detailed map of the area. He ambled along the pavement towards the City Park intent on occupying the nearest available seat in order to study it in detail. On the way, his mind dwelt on the events of the previous evening.

Connor had proved observant for the second time. He'd provided an intriguing piece of information. When he first clapped eyes on the body, Connor noticed the face looked unusual. He described it as: "Kind of weird-like...all patchy brown and white" and Connor's report made it clear it was Annie who officially identified the body, although she was in a "hell of a state" at the time, and the doctor administered a sedative immediately afterwards. He reckoned the effects of the sedative were likely to prove more lasting once the added stress of making the identification was out of the way. As was expected, most of the fingerprints on the boat related to Warren himself. There were, however, a few other prints yet to be identified. Forensic discovered traces of blood inside the boat, though it turned out not to be Warren's blood. A cast had been taken of the tyre marks found by Connor, but apart from the fact it proved a car was parked there, the marks were too indistinct to be of much use. Funnily enough though, it was Buzz who confirmed Warren's prints on the boat. Fortuitous though this may have been, why on earth, Nat mused, would the FBI have a file on him in the first place?

A limousine crawled to a halt a few feet in front of Nat. The windows were blacked out and as he attempted to pass by it, a curvaceous blonde jumped out of the front passenger door and barred his way. She smiled at him amiably enough, but as soon as she set eyes on the map, the smile froze on her face. In an instant, she snatched the map out of his hand and leapt back into the car. Nat stared after her transfixed until someone called out from the back of the car: 'It's all yours, Dug!'

It jerked Nat into action. He spun round to face a hulk of a man coming out of the rear door. The man flashed an ID card in front of him, but as Nat's eyes were focused on the hulk's sheer size at the time, the details on the card failed to register. The hulk invited him to enter the car but as Nat's natural reaction was to decline, he was unceremoniously lifted off his feet and shoved across the seat. The hulk re-entered with lips parted, revealing a number of gaps in his teeth. Nat recoiled at the sight, turning his head the other way only to be met by the steely-blue eyes of the man seated next to the offside door. The man's close-cropped fair hair, straight back and well-built chest, gave the impression of strength coupled with extreme fitness.

'Hi, Nat!' the man welcomed him. 'I'm Buzz. I've been looking forward to meeting you. Somehow, I've never quite managed it 'till now,' Nat opened his mouth. The hulk shook his head. 'As for the guy who helped you into the car,' Buzz waved a hand in the hulk's direction, 'he's known as Dug the Hug and you'll find out why if he ever gets a bear-hug on you,' Nat swung his head round again to Dug, who favoured him with yet another show of gums, 'and if you care to cast your eyes for'ard, the passenger seat is occupied by the limo's navigator, Jo, who's been plotting our journey and looks after our maps. And seated behind the wheel, you will see the limo is in the capable hands of someone who needs no introduction as far as you are concerned, Esther. A chauffeuse by any other name would be as...'

'Button-up!' she growled.

'At least,' Nat advised her smugly, 'I managed to suss that one out. I knew you weren't genuine.'

'Oh, yeah! How?'

'Quite easily, as a matter of fact. As Warren's adviser, I spent a fair amount of my time trying to persuade him to take out a policy on his life. With assets worldwide, mostly realty of one sort or another, a policy, or policies, would have helped create the wherewithal to cover the taxes arising on death. Unless he'd taken out those two policies recently, which you said he hadn't, none could have existed. That being the case, it did cross my mind that you and one of your past great presidents, George Washington, don't appear to have a lot in common.' She glowered at him in the mirror. 'But I imagine it was all in the line of duty, for Buzz and the FBI.'

Esther's glower turned into a sneer. 'As it happens, none of us work for the FBI.'

'Not to worry,' Buzz tapped Nat gently on the knee. 'All will be revealed when you meet our chief,' he glanced down at his watch, 'in just a few short minutes from now.'

The limousine turned off the main highway down a narrow road. Within a quarter of a mile, it turned off again through a pair of large metal gates, passing a couple of beefy-looking men on its way to the house at the end of a short driveway. The driver's door opened and Esther was first to be welcomed by a man dressed in uniform. Jo and Buzz followed suit and Nat was "helped" out by Dug, who was last to alight.

The sight of a military man banished any remaining qualms Nat may have had regarding his involuntary trip. The military man introduced himself as Major Homer T. Lee, aide-de-camp to General Edwin D. Halstenberg. As Nat and the Major walked towards the house together, Nat was offered an explanation.

He was told that the situation regarding the late Warren Tate had gone from bad to worse and was of extreme concern to the General. Accordingly, he'd been forced to act. Neither he (the Major) nor any of the General's staff, including those present, Allen (Buzz) Allenby, Esther

Lawrence, and Josephine Kerr, could have anticipated the inevitability of it all. The General considered that Nat's attendance at the meeting was necessary in order to assist those present in their deliberations appertaining to the circumstances shrouding and encompassing the recent series of events. According to the Major, the General was sorry to have to inconvenience Nat in this way.

Nat eyed the Major up and down.

'You're not an accountant, by any chance?'

The Major shook his head.

Buzz led the way through a side door into the house. Nat and the others followed with Dug bringing up the rear. They proceeded along a corridor towards a man whose chest and shoulders literally bulged out of his suit. At Buzz's almost imperceptible nod of the head, the man jumped aside and held open the door. Nat was ushered passed him into the room beyond.

Inside, the General was seated at the head of a table with his hand held aloft in a demonstrative manner.

Nat moved forward for a handshake but immediately realised his mistake. The General's raised hand was being used to wave him to a particular seat between Buzz and the Major. Esther slid into the seat opposite. Jo sat at a small table at the back to take notes. From the outside, Dug closed the door and Nat presumed he and his counterpart would stay there to guard the entrance to the room. A formidable couple!

The General's hand again took to the air.

'Glad you could make it, er...er...'

'Nat, sir!' Esther interjected.

'Thank you, my dear,' the General's permanently furrowed brow eased out a shade as a smile lit up his face. It returned to normal when his eyes rested once more on Nat. 'As I said, glad you could make it,' he sounded sincere with it.

'I wouldn't have missed it for the world,' Nat sounded almost as sincere.

'To put you in the picture, what I'm about to disclose is in the strictest of confidence. So before we return you to the big, bad world outside, you'll be required to put your pen to a document binding you to a state of perpetual amnesia. You'll say nothing, 'cos you'll remember nothing. Do you get my drift?' Nat indeed got his drift. 'Good man! And now I can advise you that all those in the room are members of a government agency concerned with matters of US National Security. If and when details of a confidential nature are divulged, it'll be in accordance with the dictates of necessity or advisability. But before Buzz puts his questions to you, as you were Tate's financial adviser and could well be aware of things not readily known to us, I'd like to hear from you first, especially relating to anything arising over recent weeks you may consider to be out of the ordinary.'

Nat felt honoured.

'May I first inquire, General, if Warren was also a member of your Agency?'

'You may. And he was. Employed on special assignments.'

'And would he have been working on one recently?'

'As a matter of fact, he was currently engaged on an assignment arising out of the ashes of the twin towers.'

'An anti-terrorist plan?'

'You said it, not me.'

'But would this plan have made it necessary for Warren to report to you or to your staff each day?'

'No way! Why do you ask?'

'It's just that over the past few weeks, at and around noon,

Warren's taken his fishing tackle along with him to his boat on the lake at Fortuna intent, one would imagine, on whiling away an hour on his own with his line and rod. As far as I'm aware, he never managed to catch a thing, so I wondered if in reality he might have been spending his time more profitably engaged in contacting someone upon his mobile, someone he didn't want anyone else to overhear or to know about. Someone like you, for example, or one of your Agents?'

The General stared at him aghast. 'I've issued no instructions to that effect. We'll work on that one, won't we, Buzz?'

Buzz responded with a dutiful: 'Yes, sir!' But the look on his face suggested his feathers were feeling ruffled.

Nat, on the other hand, was feeling smug. He tried hard not to show it, though not too hard.

'Also,' Nat continued, 'I believe that the Sheriff of Moose City has recently come into the possession of certain vital information. If I'm right, I've no doubt that in the course of time the information will be passed on to you. If you wish to be brought up to date now, I would suggest a phone call to the Sheriff would help to quicken the process.'

The General directed a nod at Buzz. 'Do it!'

Buzz's feathers looked even more ruffled. He grabbed the phone from the table and prodded the buttons with extra force.

'If you're trying to make a fool of us..?' he muttered grimly.

Nat didn't bat an eyelid. 'I look on murder as a serious business, especially when I get the distinct impression that I'm the one the murderer's relying on to carry the can.'

It turned out that the Sheriff was not readily available and much to his annoyance, Buzz was obliged to hang on.

During the wait, Nat's thoughts drifted back to the events of the previous evening. Apart from the fact that the anticipated epicurean disaster turned out to be a gastronomical success, whilst taking coffee after dinner, Erm and Nat attempted to discuss the case with the Sheriff who was quick to remind them that as he was no longer in charge, it was no longer his (or their) concern. But when Erm disclosed details of Warren's facial peculiarities (as described by Connor), pop was willing to take on the Sheriff's mantle once more. "As Warren's face didn't look patchy in life," he questioned, "why should it look patchy in death?" And Nat questioned police procedure when the Sheriff was unable to respond to an emergency. "In the case of homicide, who takes responsibility?" Although the Sheriff had known the deceased well, as he was out of town, it was normal for the basic formalities to be handled by the men left in charge, Connor and Elmer. Erm had pulled a face, Nat had looked pensive and the Sheriff had promised to take a closer look at the body in the morning.

When at last Buzz was able to speak to the Sheriff, the look on his face (albeit, briefly) was enough to tell Nat that the corpse lying in the morgue wasn't that of Warren Tate. Buzz shielded his mouth with his hand and reduced the volume of his voice sufficiently to make it impossible for the others in the room to overhear his conversation. Nat assumed the Sheriff was being told to keep it to himself and to keep his nose out of it as well. Buzz gave Nat (and no doubt everyone else in the room) the impression of being unconcerned. After replacing the receiver, he moved across to the General and from behind his seat spent a few moments whispering in his ear. The General's only reaction was to give an approving nod.

On his way back to his seat, Buzz leaned over Nat from behind and whispered in *his* ear too. 'Keep your trap shut tight! No info. Savvy?'

When he finally sat down, Buzz made it clear that the new evidence was no big deal and at the same time reminded those present of the funeral arrangements. But, thought Nat, how could they go ahead with the funeral arrangements knowing they're cremating the wrong body? Buzz was quick to notice the look of incredulity on Nat's face. He glared back a message, read by Nat as: "Just do as your told!" Buzz put his questions to Nat whilst the General proposed that as Nat knew Warren's personal modus operandi, he would be better placed to fill in any gaps that might arise in that direction as well as lend a hand generally.

'If you wish me to assist, General, I'm more than willing to do my bit.'

'Now is there anything we can do for you in return?'

'I must admit I would appreciate the return of my map.'

'Map?' screeched the General. 'We can do a damn sight better than some stupid map. Help us to clear up this mess and I'll give you a stack of bucks and place a medal on your chest for good measure.'

'Thank you, General. But if I can prove my worth in any way, I assure you it would not be for monetary gain. I have a score to settle and I intend to settle it come what may.'

'Good man!'

General Edwin D. Halstenberg leaned across the table and held out his hand. This time Nat knew for certain he was meant to shake it.

Chapter Ten

Spencer Wright stuck his curly, copper head and muscular shoulders further into the shrubbery. Observing the general comings and goings was fine on a fine day, but as spots of rain were beginning to fall, he knew it was only a matter of time before he was forced to seek an alternative hidey-hole. As the rate of spots increased, he viewed the heavens above through the foliage with a jaundiced eye. Within minutes, the rain had reached the bucketing stage. With determination written across his freckled face, he charged forward. At stake was the cover afforded by a number of large overhanging branches of a tall tree standing in the midst of an overgrown mass of bushes and brambles. The mass fell apart under the onslaught.

He sustained a few scratches for his trouble plus a few unwanted attachments to his hair and clothing. He wiped his face and hair with a handkerchief and peered out despondently into the gathering gloom. Out of the corner of his eye, he spotted the distant figure of a young woman. Automatically, his head swung round in her direction and his instructions to keep the driveway and the house under constant surveillance were forgotten in a flash. The feeling of despondency went as well. All the girl was wearing was a two-piece costume, a figure-hugging bikini, leaving nothing to the imagination.

What she was doing, he mused, prancing about on her own in the rain, was anybody's guess. Admittedly, the atmosphere was still warm and as she was dressed either for a bask in the sun or for a swim in the pool and as the sun was noticeable by its absence and the pool was situated on the other side of the grounds, she must have considered a bathe in the rain to be an interesting kind of alternative. Whether or not his conjecture was right, he didn't know, nor did he care. His mouth sagged open as he followed her antics. She skipped and splashed her way through the puddles, apparently heading for a series of steps leading up to a gazebo perched high on top of a man-made hillock.

Spencer could hear her calling out.

'I know you're up there, Bennett. D'you think the rain will melt you away? If you reckon it's too wet for a jog, it sure isn't too wet for a swim. If you like, we can jog along together to the pool. Come on, you muscleman, how's about it?'

But if Bennett was sheltering in the gazebo, he wasn't letting on.

Spencer thought it downright amazing that Bennett (or any other guy for that matter) could fail to respond to her call. He concluded that the noise of the rain clattering down on the roof of the gazebo was drowning out the sound of her voice.

She ran up the steps, but after reaching the bench positioned beside the steps at the halfway stage, she stopped as if to cock an ear.

A voice above was raised in anger.

'I need the money and I need it *now*!'

Although Spencer caught the words, the reply was lost in the background hiss of the rain.

'Why should I wait until after the funeral? Tell me that?'

Again, he couldn't catch the reply.

'Even if you don't agree, there's nothing you can do about it.'

But as the girl continued to gaze upwards, a figure clad in a hooded raincoat shot out of the gazebo like a scalded cat and sped down the steps towards her at great pace.

'Bennett? Is that you?' Spencer heard her call out.

But as the figure approached the step on which she was standing, it lowered its head, extended an arm, and brushed her aside on to the grass banking. She let out a piercing shriek and plunged headlong down the slope.

Spencer stifled a cry as with a dull thud she hit the ground. He broke cover and charged along the path leading to the steps of the gazebo. As he ran, his eyes were drawn to another figure belting down the steps. Through the cascading rain, he strained to detect the identity of both the first and second figures. Other than to assume that one of them was Bennett, there was no way he could identify either of them. Both were cocooned in similar waterproof outfits.

At the foot of the steps, the second figure seemed to hesitate as if drawn towards the girl stretched out by the edge of the path. The indecision didn't last long as the figure soon sped off, following closely in the other's footsteps.

Spencer took no time at all to reach the bikini-clad girl. He flung himself down beside her and checked her wrist for a pulse. He whooped for joy as he felt one. She'd suffered a nasty gash to the head and leg. He removed his jacket and shirt and draped the jacket across her body. He ripped the shirt up into bandage-size widths before wrapping them around her wounds. As he did so, the rain began to ease noticeably. From his jacket pocket, he yanked out his mobile phone and called for an ambulance.

He placed the phone on the ground and bent over her until he'd reached a level where his mouth was in line with her ear.

'Oh, honey, don't give up on me now,' he pleaded, closing his eyes as if it helped to emphasise the point. 'Especially as you're the kind of a girl I've been waiting for all my life. I just know we're made for each other. I mean to say, we share the same colour hair to start with. And I bet we share a hell of a lot of other things as well. I've called for help, though I've yet to ring in. If only I knew your name?'

'Annie!' A man shouted at him from above. 'What have *you* done to her?'

Spencer's eyes shot open. In one bound, he was back up on to his feet.

'Open your eyes,' Nat implored. 'Like it or not, I know the facts, Buzz, and you don't.'

The two were closeted together with Erm in a small porch at the entrance to the late Hank Kepler's home, a wooden veranda-styled bungalow. It stood on the lower slopes of Big Rock Ridge on the outskirts of Moose City. The trio were waiting for someone to answer the door.

'I tell you, Nat, my eyes *are* wide open,' Buzz directed a finger at them as if they were in need of identification. 'It should be as clear to you as a whippoorwill's call that Annie is about to enter her own "blue heaven". You may *think* you know the facts, but I've had it on good authority that Annie *is* Warren Tate's immediate next of kin.'

'Who by?'

'What d'you mean, who by?'

'I mean,' Nat snorted disdainfully, 'who on earth shot you this load of bull?'

'If you must know, it was Esther.'

'And where may I ask did she discover this mind-boggling piece of misinformation?'

'Where d'you think? From the horse's mouth.'

'You mean from Annie?'

'Got it in one!'

'And Esther believed her?'

'Heck! Come on, man, you know it's true. You were there at the time.'

'Strange though this may seem, Buzz, although I'm prepared to accept that Annie believes she's in line for the lion's share, I have no recollection of her making even a mention of her over-optimistic expectations in my presence,' he gazed hopefully at Erm. 'Do you recollect her saying anything like that?'

She shook her head and placed a finger across her lips. 'We're about to have company,' she whispered.

As the door opened, it revealed the friendly face of Minnie's mother, Mrs Frances Ubenski. She welcomed them warmly and bade them enter. They followed her into a small room where Minnie's greeting was confined to an upward movement of her bosom coupled with a drawn out sigh.

Most of the available space in the room was taken up by five wicker chairs, an oval table, and a closed and dented, roll-top writing desk together with a bookcase filled with a few tatty-looking books behind a cracked glass door. The walls were pinned with numerous photographs (mostly depicting Hank and his friends) and Nat assumed from this they were being seated in what was previously Hank's den.

Erm's and Nat's presence had been decreed by Buzz for "medicinal purposes" only. They were both known to Hank's wife and mother and seemed to be trusted by them, so the pair were to act as "tranquillisers", easing out any stress or tension perceived to be affecting either mother or daughter, ensuring this would relax them sufficiently to fully open up to him during the course of his interview.

Buzz introduced himself as the Officer-in-Charge of the case.

'I'm following up a number of leads,' he advised them, 'in order to track down Hank's killer. To help me to accomplish this, I need as much background information as possible concerning Hank, both inside and outside the business. For example, did Hank have any connections with the late Warren Tate or with any of the residents of the Fortuna Valley estate or. . .or . . .?'

'Or...' Erm took advantage of his hesitancy, 'did undertake any other types of work not connected with the store? I notice he was a barber in the past and wondered if he'd still kept his hand in,' as she spoke, she pointed to one of the photos on the wall.

Buzz looked daggers at her.

'Too true, he did,' said Minnie. 'But as to *his* question,' she nodded at Buzz, 'apart from the fact Hank and Nat were buddies, he'd have known some of the people at the house, like the housekeeper, Amelia, though maybe not Warren his-self. After all, Hankering supplied the house with wine. As for the photo, it's an old one of Hank and his pa with a couple of others rehearsing for an event. His pa used to run a barber's shop out east and as a kid, Hank got to know the business. In time, he picked up the tricks of the trade, including that close harmony crap. Later, after moving into the neighbourhood and when we were dating regular-like, he tried it out on me. Had the nerve to call it singing, and once we became partners in marriage, we became partners in the business too, 'specially as it was my pa who put up . . .' She rubbed her fingers together expressively, 'the folding stuff to start up Hankering. But I still let him keep his hand in every week, cutting hair for friends and for those hairy monks up on the Ridge. He called it his "charitable work". I called it a waste of effort. I kept on telling him, charity begins at home but he wouldn't listen. I ask you, what's the point of spending your time doing something for nothing?'

'Maybe it's something he loved to do?' suggested Erm.

'Are you crazy? Wait 'till you get married yourself, young lady, and you'll soon find out that love doesn't come into it. At least I knew what he was doing and where he was doing it, and I guess he couldn't get up to much mischief with Brother this and Brother that. So I did me little wifey act and gave in. It kept him happy.'

Frances looked out of the window.

'It's getting dark outside. They forecast rain. Always hits the area around the lake first before hitting us.'

As she spoke, Buzz's mobile sprang into action. He jerked it out of a pocket.

'You've got trouble, Spencer? I'll be there ASAP. OK?'

He shoved the phone back in again.

'What's up?' Nat asked.

'Annie's had an accident. Been hurt. Spencer's called for an ambulance.'

'Is she going to be alright?' Nat's concern showed.

Buzz's concern didn't. He shrugged his shoulders indifferently. 'I must go. You two can wait here.'

He jumped up, directed a vague apology to his hosts, and charged out of the room. On his way to the front door, he called out to Erm. She was to phone the Sheriff or one of his underlings and arrange to be picked up. No mention was made as to how Nat was going to get back to Fortuna.

The slam of the front door told them that Buzz had left the house.

'He's going to get wet,' Frances observed. 'It's beginning to chuck it down outside.'

'He's going to get very wet,' Erm added. 'He instructed me to drive the car. And guess who's got the keys?' She twiddled them about on the end of her little finger.

Noticeably, Minnie joined in the laughter, though it stopped abruptly when the doorbell rang. The others watched fascinated as Erm slowly stretched out her arms one at a time before raising herself up out of her chair. She even spent a few moments straightening her uniform.

The bell rang and rang. Erm strolled towards the front door and turned the latch. Buzz was standing on the doorstep, dripping wet. She extended her little finger. He grabbed the bunch of keys and departed without a word.

'Do let us know how Annie is, won't you?' she called out after him. She felt rather pleased with herself as she returned to the room. 'Serves him right, Nat, for leaving us high and dry,' she sniggered, 'and him low and wet. Should I do as the man says and ring pop? Tell him about Annie- well, as much as we know?'

Erm withdrew her handset. Whilst she was talking, Nat stood up and took a closer look at the photos dotted around the walls. Almost immediately, his eyes were drawn to a large framed one. It depicted four men all dressed alike, including a youthful looking Hank. He assumed that Hank's father was one of the two older members of the group.

'Who's this, Minnie?'

He pointed to the young man with an arm draped across Hank's shoulders.

Nat wondered how Christopher Columbus must have felt the first time he clapped eyes on America? He, too, must have experienced the drama and excitement of the occasion.

'He was one of Hank's old barbershop rowdies from back east before the prayer bug got hold of him. Arrived here a couple of years before Hank to join those bunch of wailers at the monastery. Think of it? His clean-shaven face covered in hairs. Yuk! The enlargement came from one of Hank's snaps.'

Nat was finding it hard to contain himself. 'You don't happen to remember his name?'

'Can't say that I do. Far as I'm concerned, that kind of stuff went in one ear and out the other.'

Nat managed to hide his disappointment. But he didn't blame Minnie's ears, just the bit in between. 'You wouldn't know if the original print or negative still exists?' he asked.

Though Minnie was doubtful, Frances was more optimistic.

'Wasn't that the one where the negative got lost and in the end we used the original print for the enlargement?'

'You're right, ma! Oliver said he could improve on the original print but before he could show us how good or bad it was, he lost both it and the negative. Maybe they're still somewhere around at Fortuna. Who knows?'

'Are you referring to the gardener, Oliver Jupp?'

'That's him. He did the enlargement and all the others here, too,' she waved a hand at the walls. 'It's a kind of sideline of his. Got his darkroom in a shed. Wired up for power and everything. I remember having to bawl him out at the time. Not that long ago, come to think of it. Didn't make a scrap of difference. Reckoned one moment the new print and negative were on his desk in his darkroom and the next moment they were gone. I told him if it ever happens again, it'd be more than just a print and negative he'd lose. I guaranteed he'd go from baritone to falsetto in ten seconds flat. I can tell you he never lost another thing after that.'

'When we go, Minnie, can we take the enlargement with us? We can leave you the frame, if you like, but I think it might help in the investigation if we could have it for a short time to check it out.'

'I don't get it, Nat? You can borrow the photo if you wants. But what makes you think Oliver had anything to do with Hank's death?'

As Erm was in the final throes of her phone call, Minnie's last words registered with her loud and clear.

'Yeah, Nat, what's with the gardener, Oliver Jupp?'

'I'm not saying he has anything to do with it, but just take a peek at the photograph, enlarged by Oliver himself and at the man standing next to Hank with an arm around his shoulder. Tell me what you think?'

'Holy Moses!' she screeched.

'Holy Moses!' he screeched. 'What-on-earth made you hit him?' Buzz viewed Spencer from the other side of the utility room with a disapproving eye. The room was attached to the kitchen area of the Fortuna residence. Buzz rubbed a towel through his hair and slung it across the room for Spencer to finish drying off.

'Put yourself in my shoes, Buzz. What was I meant to think when I jumped up and found the guy standing there was called Bennett? I was in a state of shock at the time, not knowing if the girl was going to pull through and all that, and she'd been calling out *his* name.'

'Spencer? Your job was to survey the house and driveway, not the area in the opposite direction.'

'They were peeled the other way just in case.'

'Just in case of what?'

'Just in case anything happened to her, and as it happens, my vigilance was rewarded. Something *did* happen to her.'

Buzz held his head in his hands. 'Spencer,' he implored, 'just get on with it.'

'I know I shouldn't have done it, but you must admit it was an easy mistake to make. Still, with all those muscles you'd have thought he'd have put up more of a fight. Not just lay there on the ground, moaning and groaning. When the paramedic guys arrived in the ambulance, they couldn't tell who was in need of help more, him or her. And another thing how was I to know the girl, Annie, was a squeamish kind-of-a broad? It was the sight of her own blood and not her injuries that made her pass out in the first place. Then as soon as they revived her, she took one look at her leg all bandaged up with my torn shirt...and guess what? She went and damned well passed out again. I reckon it was lucky she couldn't see the bandages around her head, otherwise the paramedic guys would have had their work cut out and no mistake. But the good news is there were no bones broken and her wounds turned out to be not as bad as they looked. When at last they hauled Bennett up on to his feet, he became abusive-like. Reckoned he could have me for assault. I told him, it'd be a good way of finding out what Annie really feels about him if it became public knowledge as to how well he *didn't* defend himself. It sure made him lighten up in a hurry. He was OK after that. Assured me that he would never harm Annie, and according to him, he was on one of his jogs when it started to rain. Took shelter in a shed. But later on, he decided to risk it in case Annie was still waiting for him. They'd arranged to meet and jog to the gazebo together. He said they'd planned to get down to some really hard exercise inside. I wouldn't have minded him telling me that but for the way he said it, all suggestive-like. Point is though, the gardening guy, Jupp, was sheltering in the shed with him. So Bennett has a cast-iron alibi. Also, according to Rosie, Amelia Cadogan's assistant, Annie was set for a swim in the pool and a sun bathe afterwards. As the heavens opened up with a vengeance and the sun had lost its shine, she was all on edge when Annie failed to show and went out in search of her. But when she heard the ambulance's siren blasting away and discovered it'd come to collect Annie, it was panic stations. She fussed over her like a mother hen over her chick and pleaded to go along with her to the hospital. At the time, I'd yet to question Bennett, and I reckoned it might help Annie if Rosie went along.'

'And is that it?'

'No, not exactly. You see I've been on tenterhooks ever since. Had to ring the hospital to see how she was getting on. Even if the cuts and bruises weren't serious in themselves, she could have been suffering from internal injuries not obvious to the paramedic guys. Or. . . or what if the head injury has affected the brain?'

'Whose brain are we talking about?'

'Hers, of course,' Buzz choked back a guffaw. 'But the great news is that Annie's due to be discharged within the hour and I kind of wondered if it'd be OK for me to go and pick her up?'

'If Bennett doesn't beat you to it.'

'Then it's best if I go soon.'

'Sooner the better. It'll enable you to interview the victim. With any luck you might discover who did it. But before you go, as you took your jacket off to cover her up and as the jacket's designed to take your gun and communicator, you'd better check they're both dry and still in working order. And check your clothes, too, whilst you're about it.'

Spencer stretched out a hand and turned on the phone. 'Yep! That one's OK.'

'What about your clothes?'

They were draped over a radiator.

'Dry as a bone. I must admit, Tate's clothes are a perfect fit.'

'That's 'cos Tate was about the same size and build as us. Except unlike us, he was rich and all the ladies loved him.'

'I'm beginning to dislike him.'

'Join the club.'

'Just as well he's dead.'

Buzz kept his mouth shut, but hoped to bring Spencer into the fold in time for the funeral. With Tate on the loose and with a strong indication that others (and especially others in his department) were involved, an outside assistant he could trust might well prove to be the safest bet.

'How about your gun?'

'No problem there, Buzz.'

'How d'you know without checking it?'

'I made sure it didn't get wet.'

'How?'

'I rammed it down the inside of my underpants and let it dangle between my legs.'

'Wasn't that dangerous?'

'Nope! I made damn sure the safety catch was on.'

'I mean, Spencer, couldn't it have fallen out?'

'No way! I tied a strip of my shirt around my waist inside my underpants and with the length over, tied the gun to it. It just stuck out a bit, that's all.'

From inside the kitchen, Amelia Cadogan couldn't help but overhear him.

'I might have guessed,' she muttered to herself, 'it was too good to be true.'

Chapter Eleven

The teenager wrapped an arm around the young girl's waist and squeezed.

'Be-have yourself, Leroy.'

But Leroy knew he was on to a good thing.

His dark brown eyes lit up in lustful anticipation as his black hand moved on to the more supple parts of the girl's white and shapely body and uncovered an area of sufficient sensitivity to raise in her a high-pitched giggle of excitement. When he calculated the giggles had reached their peak, he reckoned it was time to pop the ultimate question.

'How's about it, Myrt?'

Without hesitation, Myrt flung herself backwards on to the grass.

Just as rapidly, she rebounded back up again.

'Pis-tach-io!' she screeched. 'The damn grass is pee-wet. Just look at the state of my dress?'

He stared unsympathetically at the blotches.

'It'll dry out, Myrt.'

'Yeah! But it could leave dirty marks.'

'If it does, I'll buy you a new one.'

'You bet your sweet life you will.'

'Why don't I take off my shirt for you to lie on?'

'And make it soaking wet, too?'

'OK! What if I place both of my hands flat on the grass under each of your . . .er butt-er-cups? That should do the trick, shouldn't it?'

'Not even you, Leroy, have enough hands to protect the rest of my dress as well, though there sure are times when I can't tell the difference between you and a randy octopus.'

'What d'you suggest I do?'

'I suggest you . . .' she eyed him up and down. 'Go find a nice dry spot, express-like, else we'll call it a day.'

Leroy was beginning to feel cheated.

Myrt held her head of long, blonde curls high in the air before turning round and marching off back towards the path.

As he sheepishly followed on, his mind was working overtime. And it took him only a few strides to come up with an answer.

He called out after her: 'I've got it, Myrt. Ease up, will you?'

She eased up a fraction.

As he caught up with her, he grabbed her waist from behind and puffed out his cheeks as if out of breath.

'You don't want to get me..' he made gasping noises in her ear, 'all tuckered out, do you, Myrt, beforehand?'

Apparently, she couldn't care less.

'D'you know what's on the other side of the fence?'

She told him that she couldn't care less.

'It belonged to a guy who got himself killed recently. And he had a summerhouse built only a few yards in from here, all dry and cosy-like.'

'If you think, even for a sec, I'm going to clamber over an . . .' she waved her hand at it in disgust, '. . . obstacle course, you must be out of your tiny mind.'

'No need! Some helpful guy's gone and cut a hell of a chunk out of the chain-link for us to get through,' he pointed to a clump of bushes. 'Over there, behind that lot. You'll be able to sail through it...no sweat.'

'How d'you know that?'

'My buddy, Ricky, wised me up on it. He and his girl, Babs, found it when they were doing their thing together, you know, at one with nature and all that crap. At the time, they were into wild and rare flowers, 'specially the ones found in woods like the woods on the other side of the fence. That's when they came across the summerhouse. They thought it too risky to stay outside.'

'What's risky about that?'

'They could have trodden on one of 'em without knowing it. You sure need an eagle eye and a dainty foot to do their thing. Ricky may have an eagle eye, but his feet tend to spread out over a wide area. Inside the summerhouse, they were able to spot most of the interesting stuff through the windows, without Ricky putting his foot in it...or on it.'

'How damned lucky can you get?'

'Yeah! I guess they were lucky.'

'Not *them*. *You!*

We must have passed at least a dozen similar bushes bordering the fence on our way here, yet you picked that one out in an instant. Tell me, how d'you manage to do it?'

'Ricky detailed its position real good.'

'Oh, yeah! Pull the other one.'

Myrt flashed her eyes up and down a couple of times and headed for the back of the bushes.

'Well, come on, Leroy?' she called out. 'Stop dragging your heels. I reckon it's best all round if I *don't* find out what you've been up to.'

He feigned an expression of wounded innocence as he made his way after her through the gap in the fence.

'What happens if someone spots us?' she said.

'We'll make out we're lost.'

'What if they don't believe us?'

'We'll make a run for it.'

'And what if we can't out-strip them?'

'No prob there, Myrt. I came first in this year's school sprint.'

'Thanks a bundle!'

As they approached the large wooden and glass structured building, Leroy bounded forward to open the door for Myrt to enter. For a moment or two, the couple surveyed the interior.

There were windows on three sides, making it almost impossible for anyone inside not to be seen by anyone outside. On one side, the branches of the trees were touching the windows, though not enough to prevent anyone looking in.

'All the seats are padded.'

Myrt was impressed.

'And there's a table, cupboards, lights, and it's been wired for power and sound.'

Leroy was equally impressed.

Myrt gently stretched herself out on one of the bench-type seats.

Leroy far less gently stretched himself out on top of her.

The kiss that followed lasted several minutes. And in a repeat performance, his limpet-like hands wandered up the back of her legs and wrapped themselves around the tops of her scanty knickers. As he made efforts to remove them, she pressed her legs hard against the bench's upholstery, extracting a groan or two from an increasingly frantic Leroy.

Unlike him, she was enjoying the struggle.

Whilst he soldiered on, she gazed up at the wooden-beamed ceiling above her head and allowed her eyes to wander aimlessly around the room. Eventually, they settled on a side window where the branches of the trees were making noises as they scraped across the glass. As she looked, the branches parted abruptly and in their place the face of a man appeared with his nose pressed hard against the glass.

The scream that followed shot Leroy up into the air. He landed face downwards on the wooden floor. His curse was almost as loud as her scream.

With his hands gingerly clasped around the affected area of his body, he picked himself up. He glared at her with watering eyes.

'What the flaming bucc-an-eer do you think you're playing at?'

She pointed a trembling finger at the window.

'We've got ourselves a peeping Tom.'

His eyes followed the direction of her finger.

'Leave it to me, Myrt,' he bawled. 'I'll soon put paid to his little game.'

He charged off in his underpants to confront the offender.

The window was situated on the least accessible side of the summerhouse. In order to be in a position to grab hold of the man, Leroy was forced to thrust himself forward through a maze of shrubbery, saplings, and the overhanging branches of taller trees.

On the inside, Myrt watched petrified as the face began to slide down the glass. Leroy watched equally petrified as the man collapsed in a heap at his feet. Without the weight of his body to keep them apart, the branches previously scraping the window rebounded back with a vengeance. Leroy stuck out an arm to fend them off. With horror, he noticed some of the branches had spattered the glass with red spots.

Myrt's shrieks resounded throughout the timber framework. She could see the same coloured spots spattered across most of Leroy's face and upper body. He stared back at her covered in blood.

Chapter Twelve

In between the soulful sounds emanating from the organ, an intermittent sob echoed around the chapel. Annie was seated in the pew with a paper tissue clutched tightly in her hand and a packet of the same resting on her lap. She was flanked on either side by attentive consolers. One in the guise of the FBI Agent, Spencer Wright, and the other in the guise of the late Warren Tate's confidant and chauffeur, Bennett McCorquodale. Sitting immediately behind her was a third attentive consoler, Rosie Witherspoon, directing into Annie's ear such words of comfort as: 'there, there, me love...there, there'.

Upon their arrival, Erm and Nat sought out Annie to express, as Nat put it, their condolences on her sad loss. Erm hovered in the background dressed in a tight, sophisticated, black chiffon skirt and top especially acquired for the occasion from Fort Jackson's finest departmental store.

When Nat first set eyes on her new rig-out, he was quick to tell her how stunning she looked in it. He told her that if the deceased could see her now, he too would have approved of it for certain.

As they entered the chapel, Nat was keen to cast an eye left and right to see if he was actually approving of it in the flesh.

Once Nat had completed his expressions of sympathy on behalf of the two of them, Erm promptly jerked him away in the direction of the vacant seats she'd spotted in the pew at the back. She reckoned that the seats were as far out of earshot of Annie's sobs and Rosie's "there there's" as they could be. Erm beckoned him to go ahead of her and he slid across next to the only other occupant of the pew, Amelia Cadogan. Erm seated herself on the other side of him.

'A thorn between two roses,' Nat whispered.

In a hushed voice, Amelia told Nat how shocked she was to hear the dreadful news about the death of Doctor Cornell. She proffered an opinion that the man must have been up to no good, especially after what she'd seen and heard at the bank. But she felt that no man deserved to be stabbed all that many times, 'however bad he's been'.

'One hard stab in the back is enough to make one's point, don't you think?'

'I imagine the victim would have preferred the murderer to have missed the point altogether.'

Feeling confused, Nat paused for a moment to marshal his thoughts.

'But what was it you saw and heard at the bank?'

'Surely, you can't have forgotten already? That rogue of a man, Chester Cornell, making out he was you. Even tried to put on your rather nice educated accent. Nowhere near convincingly enough as far as I was concerned. But all the same, I guess he still managed to pull the wool over the State Union's manager's eyes.'

'Of course I remember, Amelia. How on earth could I forget? Someone having the blood-blooming cheek to impersonate me.' Nat's hushed voice began to lose its hush. 'But how do you know it was Chester Cornell?'

'I was there when the Doc opened the account. There was another man with him at the time, dressed in a suit. Though somehow he looked out of place in it. Never seen him before in my life. Though definitely in on it.'

'Never mind *him*. The point is *you* were there!'

It sounded as if the rest of the mourners shushed him in unison. Erm eyed Nat up and down disapprovingly. She reminded him that the purpose of attending a funeral wasn't to raise the dead but to pay ones last respects.

In more reverent tones, Nat resumed. 'We were living under the same roof, Amelia. So why didn't you tell me?'

For once, Amelia's normal unflappability showed signs of flapping. 'How was I to know? I did what I thought was the right thing to do at the time and reported it, as one has a duty to do, to the Sheriff.'

'*You reported it?*'

A further sea of shushes greeted him for a second time, though he managed to control himself sufficiently to reduce the volume before the end of the sentence. Even so, the final word came out in the form of an extended hiss.

'To the Sh-sh-eriff?'

'What's going on, Nat?' Erm twisted her head and body forward and glared at him.

'Apparently your father,' he fairly spat out the word, 'the senior custodian of law and order in Moose City received a report from Amelia that she not only saw who it was opened up the bank account in my name but she actually overheard the conversation going on at the time between the impostor and a bank official,'

'You mean pop's known all along?'

'That's about the size of it. And guess who the impostor is?'

'You don't mean..?'

'Yes, I *do* mean that philistine of the medical profession, Doctor Chester Cornell. Why-on-earth, Erm,' he gazed intensely into her deep blue eyes searching for an answer, 'didn't your father tell me? What made him keep it from me?'

'More to the point, what reason could he have for keeping his daughter in the dark as well?'

They both turned their heads and stared incredulously at the

Sheriff seated with his wife, Siobhan, across the aisle. The Sheriff returned their stare with a cordial grin. This induced in each of them a scowl of condemnation. In an instant, the Sheriff's manner changed from one of relative serenity to one of sheer bewilderment.

Siobhan leaned across her husband to give her daughter and, in her opinion, her daughter's most acceptable gentleman friend a warm smile. They returned the warm smile with extra warmth, adding further to the Sheriff's state of confusion.

Outside, Buzz appeared from around the back of the building in time to see the hearse draw up at the chapel gates, closely followed by a black limousine. Esther Lawrence slid her shapely legs out of the limousine and placed her fashionable black shoes on to the tarmac.

Originally, Annie, as chief mourner, was invited to occupy the funeral directors' limousine together with any friends or associates she may wish to accompany her. The limousine was to follow on in tandem with the hearse from the Chapel of Rest to the crematorium. But she declined the invitation on the grounds that she couldn't bear to think of 'Warren's lifeless body' being carried inside the vehicle in front of her. Nat wondered how she would cope with the funeral rites themselves with the coffin resting on its obsequial stand in full view - almost within touching distance of her - throughout the entire ceremony? Consequently, apart from Esther, the only other occupant of the limousine was the lawyer, Max Goldbloom. Nat later discovered that his car had broken down and as he was in need of a lift, Esther was willing to act as the Good Samaritan. Nat considered she was not so much acting the Good Samaritan, but demonstrating her astuteness at seizing a golden opportunity to pump the lawyer for information.

As he passed by, Buzz hollered out instructions to Esther to get in and grab a pew. At pace, he disappeared through the chapel's outer doors and into the vestibule. Once inside the chapel itself, he came to a halt and stood surveying the congregation. As soon as he'd spotted his prey, he flew down the aisle with talons extended.

'Where the hell-eck have you been?'

Spencer squirmed embarrassingly in his seat. 'Annie needs me, Buzz.'

'Does she, now!'

'She's taken it badly, Buzz.'

'Has she, now!'

'See for yourself?'

He stared down at her, poker-faced.

'You'll find it's best, Annie, to get it off your chest...' She blinked up at him through tear-stained eyelashes, '..before the ceremony starts in earnest.'

No further persuasion was necessary. Her sobs rose to wailing proportions.

Buzz leaned over and whispered in her ear. 'If you carry on like this, how will you and the other mourners be able to hear all those nice things they're going to say about him? Why not give your nose a good blow? Remember, we're all thinking of him.'

'Even you, Buzz?'

'Me, especially!'

He beckoned Spencer to join him.

'I need to borrow Spencer for a moment, Annie. He'll be back with you again before you know it.'

Spencer mumbled a few words of comfort to Annie.

Bennett's beam was broad and genuine. 'Not to worry, me ol' buddy-boy,' he said. 'Rest assured she'll be in safe hands with me.'

Spencer not only felt far from assured but also took great

exception to being referred to as Bennett's "ol' buddy-boy".

On the surface, one look from Buzz seemed sufficient to restrain any thoughts of a retaliatory nature. In truth, this was entirely due to the fact that the straight finger Spencer intended to thrust up Bennett's nose was being held down by Buzz in a vice-like grip from behind.

A voice from the rear of the chapel sent them scampering back up the aisle. The congregation was being asked to rise.

On their way, the two were forced to negotiate a clergyman, a coffin, four pall-bearers, as well as Esther. The latter avoided contact by plonking herself down beside Erm. Both aimed pecks at the other's cheek.

As Buzz and Spencer brushed by the clergyman, he was rocked back on his heels and seemed to lose the drift of his opening incantation. As it happened, for the most part, the organ was playing loud enough for it to go unnoticed.

The two men hurried to a door marked AUTHORISED ENTRY ONLY and passed through it into the rear of the chapel. Buzz waved a Letter of Authority under the noses of the usual attendants and directed them to "stay put" in an ante-room until they (their replacements, pro tem,) had 'put to rest' the 'dearly departed' in the crematorium's incinerator. For their part, Buzz and Spencer, waited patiently and in silence for the funeral service to end.

In the chapel itself, once the coffin was in place on its obsequial stand, the pall-bearers discreetly withdrew to the outside of the building. The stand was covered on three sides by velvet curtains and Buzz and Spencer were positioned on the other side of the split central curtain. It acted as a screen for the coffin to move through on a specially designed travelator during the concluding part of the ceremony.

After a robust rendition of a number of traditional hymns by the mourners and the delivery by the chapel's resident cleric of a less than robust eulogy together with prayers, the participants were faced with a histrionic performance given by none other than Bennett McCorquodale on the life and virtues of the late Warren Tate.

According to him, the deceased could do no wrong. More to the point, he'd "done no wrong" throughout the entire length of his "industrious and charitable life". It was a veritable example to them all.

Behind the curtain, the two expressed their feelings in mime. They mouthed a number of expletives and grimaced repeatedly.

As the ceremony progressed, Spencer brought to Buzz's notice the fact that although the sound of Annie's sobs and Rosie's "there, there's" could still be heard above the cleric's oratory, the proximity of the coffin to Annie herself hadn't noticeably extended her grief in any shape or form. Spencer thought it was a good sign. Buzz nodded back but kept his thoughts to himself.

Once the service had reached its climax, the cleric pressed the pertinent button to send the coffin gliding along its travolator through the split curtain.

Buzz and Spencer were waiting for it on the other side, each equipped with a screwdriver.

They pushed the coffin on to a static stand and proceeded to remove the lid.

'Why don't we dump the lot in the furnace?' suggested Spencer helpfully. 'Save a hell of a lot of effort.'

"Cos the most essential thing is to ensure the weight feels lifelike (ha! ha!). Can't risk anyone raising questions about it, can we? And that made it necessary to use a specially designed metal skeleton of the correct weight and size, designed by one of our agents, as a matter of fact. Trouble is metal has a habit of staying put even if in shapeless lumps. Hence the reason for removing it. As it is, we're going to have our work cut out trying to create sufficient ash to cover Warren's body size. That's why we've been humping those old animal bones around.' He waved a hand in the direction of two large suitcases on the floor.

'All the same, it still seems a kind of waste of time. Why couldn't we have put the bones in the coffin in the first place?'

'It's not just a question of getting the weight right, Spencer, we can't have the contents rattling around inside, and one thing's for sure this skeleton can be used over and over again. Remember? Ours is not to reason why, ours is but to do as instructed.'

'If *you* say so, Buzz.'

As Spencer stared innocently into space, Buzz eyed him with a mixture of suspicion and irritation. Spencer's thoughts, however, were centred on the information recently disclosed to him by the General's aide-de-camp, Major Lee. He let out that Buzz's Bunsen burner was synonymous with his pastime of metal work. The skeleton was *his* baby. Spencer inquired as to how many times *his* baby was likely to be used by the Pentagon at a funeral where the corpse was in need of an understudy? The Major's reply was too ambiguous to comprehend.

Between them, Buzz and Spencer lifted the skeleton out of the coffin and laid it out horizontally on the floor with its metal spine and buttocks resting underneath. Spencer could see how much Buzz relished the task of taking it to pieces and, in the circumstances, felt he should stand aside and allow Buzz the privilege of playing with his own brainchild.

First, the weighty band fixed around the abdomen and waist was unclipped. Next, the buttocks, legs and feet were parted from the torso, neck and head. Buzz went to great lengths to explain how the band not only kept everything together but also anchored the skeleton in place and prevented it from moving around inside the coffin.

The yawn that followed was wide and long.

Spencer was told in no uncertain manner to "get his finger out" and get the cases opened up and their contents emptied into the coffin. After that, he was instructed to spread the bones about inside it in order to ensure that nothing protruded above the level of the lid.

Buzz himself opted to fill both cases with the various parts of the skeleton.

Together, they screwed the lid of the coffin back in place. They also removed all the brass handles and fixings. These were left in a heap on top of the static stand for the attendants to deal with on their return.

On the call of "heave-ho and hup", they yanked the coffin back on to the travelator and sent it on the final leg of its journey. As it passed a certain point on the way, the doors of the incinerator swung open and the coffin and its contents were sent plunging into the depths of the inferno. Once inside, the doors automatically closed again.

Buzz grabbed a case and headed for the exit. Spencer grabbed the other one only to discover he'd been handed the short straw. He reckoned his case must have included the weighty band as well as a good half of the metal skeleton. He swore under his breath as he staggered off after him. And when Buzz called in on the attendants in the ante-room, Spencer took the opportunity to plonk his case down on the floor pretty smartish.

Buzz told the attendants that he and his fellow mourner had paid their respects to the deceased, though not their last respects. Their faith was such that they truly believed that one day they'd come face to face with the deceased once more, "provided the good Lord heeds our most heartfelt prayers". Finally, Buzz instructed the attendants to recommence their duties as from "the next stiff in line".

His remarks gave Spencer something to grin about as he faced up to the strain of humping the case to the safety of the boot of their car. He lurched forward with his jaw set and eyes fixed unwaveringly ahead, following in Buzz's wake.

Fortunately, the majority of the mourners had departed to the other side of the chapel to view the wreaths and flowers displayed in the Garden of Remembrance. Only four mourners were in Spencer's line of vision and three of those were engaged in a heated argument. All of them were too preoccupied to notice his or Buzz's presence.

As the non-participator in the controversy, Siobhan was determined to pour vocal oil on troubled waters.

'We've only just come out of the Chapel of God,' she pleaded, 'so let's have less blare and more of the "Lord forgive us as we seem unable to show respect to the member of your flock who's just passed over to the other side".'

'I'll tell you one more time..' the Sheriff let rip.

'If you must blow your top, honey,' Siobhan interjected, her voice raised, 'blow it somewhere else. We are within earshot of the Garden of Remembrance and those standing in it will not want to be reminded of the kind of human frailties you're at present depicting; a loud mouth and pig-headedness.'

'As you both seem inclined to be a mite on the deaf side as well as a mite on the dumb side..' the Sheriff continued unabated, 'Amelia Cadogan *did not*, I repeat, *did not* contact me nor did she tell me about what she saw and heard in the bank.'

Siobhan raised her arms in frustration. As Siobhan's message had already percolated through to Erm and Nat, they thought better of it and kept their mouths shut. Their unwillingness to extend the argument took the heat out of the situation, and they succeeded where Siobhan failed.

The Sheriff's follow-up question was almost subdued.

'O-Ka-ay?'

Siobhan spotted Amelia returning from an inspection of the floral tributes. 'Why don't you ask the lady herself? I mean, quiet and peaceful like, Oswald. That'll settle the issue once and for all.'

Nat immediately raised a hand and brought Amelia to a halt.

'I'm sorry to trouble you,' he said, 'but it would be most helpful if you could reiterate what you disclosed to me inside the chapel, about seeing Doctor Cornell at the bank. The Sheriff would be interested to hear what you have to say.'

'But the Sheriff already knows about it. So what's the point?'

'*No I don't!*' In an effort to retain his composure, the Sheriff pressed four fingers and a thumb deep into the knuckles of his other hand. 'The point *is*, Amelia, you've yet to tell me anything.'

'I agree I didn't tell you personally. As I recollect, I was much too busy at the time, what with the shopping and the cooking. It's never-ending, you know.' As she stared at him, a puzzled frown creased her brow. 'Do you mean to say you never received my message?'

'Never!'

'To whom, Amelia, did you entrust your message?' Nat inquired.

'I gave specific instructions to Hardy. I know it's not his real name but I call him that as he's got to be hardy to work out of doors, don't you think? And with a name like that, what else could it be?'

'You mean it was Oliver...Oliver Jupp?'

The "yes" was barely audible, though her raised eyebrows were most expressive.

The Sheriff's eyebrows responded likewise.

Nat wanted to know when she spoke to Oliver?

'It was after poor Warren's death. It was that that jogged my memory, and it aroused my suspicions too, especially as he was the doctor who attended Warren at the time of his death.'

Oswald Kramer scratched his bald pate.

'Why didn't you check on it later to make sure he'd passed on your message?'

'I assure you, Sheriff, if I could have done I would have done, but I needed to concentrate my mind in the kitchen. It's a well known fact that expertly prepared food helps to raise the spirits enormously, and I was determined to do my bit for Annie.'

As she spoke, the Sheriff felt a sharp pain in the pit of his stomach.

The stupid woman had brought on one of his dyspeptic bouts.

Chapter Thirteen

The beneficiaries were seated around the lawyer's desk. On each of their faces was etched an air of anxiety. On tenterhooks they awaited the details of their respective inheritances. As the sole non-beneficiary present, Nat was free of such anxieties. Having discussed the matter with Warren in the past, he was conversant with the outline of the will. Nat's view was that for most of them seated in the room their inheritances would come as somewhat of a let- down (if not a complete shock), unlikely to produce much in the way of inner jubilation and, he reckoned, that the usual outward display of sorrow might well leave a bitter taste in some of their mouths.

Nat excluded Annie from the usual outward display of sorrow on the grounds that her grief at Warren's departure was genuine in the extreme. Nevertheless, he reckoned she still would be expecting to feel an inner glow of hereditable gratification. She could be in for a rude awakening.

Other than for those due to benefit under the terms of the will, only Nat was given permission to attend Max Goldbloom's reading of Warren Tate's last Will and Testament at his offices in Fort Jackson and whilst the lawyer still remained reticent, Nat mulled over the significance of Oliver Jupp's absence. Yesterday, Jupp had failed to show up at the funeral, and today he'd also failed to show up for the reading of the will. Annie disclosed the fact that Oliver had received a phone call on the morning of the funeral and left soon afterwards without saying a word.

Max Goldbloom took a final puff of his cigar before crushing it into his over-filled onyx ashtray. A cloud of cigar ash rose into the air above his desk. He pursed his lips and blew it out of the way. Whereupon he leaned back in his chair and patiently waited for the coughing to subside before lighting up again.

'We've delayed proceedings long enough for Jupp to show, though I guess it's understandable in the circumstances, so I'll make a start by giving you an outline of my client's will as it effects each of you as beneficiaries.'

'Understandable, Max?' Nat posed the question. 'Do you mean it's understandable bearing in mind the authorities are looking for him? Or do you mean it's understandable as you're aware of, or have an inkling, as to the reason for his absence? And that perhaps you happen to know where he is?'

'I'm here to read the will, Nat, not to go into Jupp's personal affairs.'

And that was that!

Nat listened attentively (as did the others) to the lawyer as he read out those parts of the will applicable to the beneficiaries together with an occasional explanation he deemed fit.

Max summed up the position at the end.

'I guess that gives you some idea as to what was in my client's mind when he made out his will, and to his reasons for splitting the pecuniary bequests at five thousand dollars apiece for some and ten thousand dollars apiece for others. In addition, there are a few specific objets d'art for "the ladies in his life". I will let the ladies concerned have a list of those items individually inherited. They being: Annie, Amelia and Rosie . . .' The sound of Nat's sharp intake of breath forced him into hurrying the rest of the sentence. 'before-they-go. I regret there will be no continuity of employment for any of Warren's staff. The estate will cover pay and costs for the next seven days only and after that, the residuary legatee will take charge, but I can't hold at much hope there.'

'Why not, Max?' Annie scowled back at him. 'I'm more than

willing to take them on.'

'Most generous of you, I'm sure. As long as you realise you'll have to employ them some place else.'

'Why on earth should I?'

'The residuary legatee happens to be Warren's immediate next of kin.'

'And she is sitting right in front of you, Max.'

'You are. She isn't.'

'Who isn't?'

'The residuary legatee.'

'But *I'm* the main thingy, aren't I?'

'No, Annie. If you consider the "main thingy" to be the one who inherits the bulk of the estate, it's not you.'

As Nat predicted, the news hit Annie hard and most of the others as well regarding their particular share of the spoils, as well as losing their jobs. In Bennett's case, he was due to receive (as he later put it) "a measly five thousand dollars" for spending years of his life "at Warren's beck and call". Oliver was due to receive a similar amount.

The ladies came off best as their cash bequests amounted to ten thousand dollars each.

'If it's not me, who else can it be?' Annie looked and sounded put out.

For a moment or two, the lawyer eyed her up and down in silence.

'You seem to forget that Warren was a married man, albeit separated from his wife. Nonetheless, the lady in question, Su Jiang-Tate, is still legally his wife and therefore his immediate next of kin. I gather she's due to take up residency at the Fortuna house any time now.'

'Surely the will can't apply to a wife who's been doing her own thing somewhere else, *and* more than likely doing it with someone else, and doing it in some far-flung corner of the world? For ages, too! Surely, Warren must have made out his will prior to them separating and just forgot to change it afterwards?'

'Not so! The will's dated three years ago and his wife left him a year before that. That's a year before the will was signed.'

'Su Jiang? Sounds kind of oriental to me.'

'That's because she *is* oriental. And that you will discover when you come face to face with her next week.'

'Was there a codicil to the will?' Nat piped up. 'Anything added to it at a later stage?'

'I can assure you, Nat, nothing's been added to the will since the day it was signed.'

'Most interesting!'

'Most interesting?' Annie looked daggers at him. 'What d'you mean by that? I can tell you, Nat, it's not most interesting to me. I think it's nothing short of a calamity.' She bent her head and fumbled up the sleeve of her dress as if in search of a handkerchief. She was unsuccessful in her quest and instead wiped a finger gently across each eye. With a touch of exasperation, the lawyer grabbed hold of the packet of tissues on his desk and tossed them on to her lap. 'Tha-anks, Max. Warren more or less promised I'd inherit Fortuna. He told me so a number of times.'

As both Bennett and Rosie remained stuck in their seats, Nat felt obliged to act. He stepped forward and from behind her seat, placed a hand gently on each of her shoulders.

'I didn't mean to upset you, Annie. But you did say it was only a "more-or-less promise". How did Warren actually put it?'

'He said he'd leave me what he treasures most of all. What else could it be other than that of his lovely house and grounds?'

'Heavens preserve us!' Max stared at her in astonishment. 'Warren wasn't referring to his house and grounds, Annie. He was referring to the nude statuette he kept on a plinth inside his bedroom door. That's the thing he treasured most of all. The objet d'art he left you in his will.'

Nat gazed down at her like a priest about to exhort a member of his flock to face adversity with courage. He felt concern. He felt compassion. He laid his hands on her head and as a result found himself saying such improbable words of sympathy he never would have thought in a million years could have found their way passed his lips.

'There, there! There, there!'

To make matters worse, it prodded Rosie into action. She bounded out of her seat and brushed him aside. Nat left her to it and headed for the door.

'I must go, Max,' he called out. 'Thanks for inviting me.'

'Not me, Nat. You'll have to thank Warren for that. Though the invitation dates back to the instructions he gave me round about the time he made the will.'

'But before I depart, tell me, do you really have any idea as to what's become of Oliver Jupp?'

'I can't say for sure, but if one of your old English definitions of a possible location is of help, I suggest you try the local hostel for travellers.'

Max grinned at him as if he'd cracked a joke. Nat returned the grin in order to hide his ignorance and irritation (funny ha-ha it was not). Though his irritation vanished as soon as he clapped eyes on Erm standing next to Spencer outside, and yet again, her plain clothes were anything but plain. She was kitted out in a gold coloured, cowgirl-styled skirt and top with leather flaps and tassels. Ever since she'd decided to remove her trousers (as it were) and renew her acquaintance with skirt, he considered that her ensemble had gone up from eye-catching to eye-boggling proportions. But he wasn't complaining.

She greeted him with a 'Hi!' and Spencer beamed a welcome as well.

Spencer's instruction was to obtain as much information from Nat concerning the contents of the will as soon as Nat appeared.

Initially, the fact that Bennett and Annie would be closeted together in the same room gave Spencer cause for concern, but as soon as Annie agreed to let him accompany her to the lawyer's office and back, all became sweetness and light. As a result of a course of action agreed between Erm and her father, she too was waiting for Nat outside the building. Their plan was to co-operate with Buzz (as they're duty bound to do) but she would continue the investigation surreptitiously.

Erm was keen to get in first and Nat was keen to take a closer look at her in her new rig-out.

'You're needed,' he informed Spencer. 'By Annie.'

Spencer was out of sight in a flash.

'Well, that's dealt with him. Now it's your turn, partner.'

Nat twirled the ends of an imaginary moustache suggestively.

'But supposing someone sees us?'

'There's hardly anybody about.'

'The sidewalk *is* open to the public.'

'Bugger the public!'

'Well, if that's the way you feel, I'll leave you to it. But I reckon you could be biting off more than you can chew.'

'Ouch!' Nat winced.

'It's up to you?'

Nat gave his imaginary moustache another twirl. 'My motto is to strike while the iron's hot.'

'And my motto is to be wised up first and struck later.'

'But my iron could have gone cold by then?'

'It'll soon warm up again,' she told him, 'once I've switched the power back on.'

'And when do you propose to do that?'

'Anytime when I'm good and ready.'

Nat asked if she could be a little more precise.

'Thank your lucky stars. Anytime's better than no time at all.'

'True enough!'

They linked arms and giggled like a couple of teenagers as they moved off towards the multi-storey car park. Nat did as Erm directed and promptly filled her in as to the contents of Warren's will and the imminent arrival of his estranged wife, Su Jiang.

'But as you know, there's still a number of loose ends to unravel relating to the events of the day Warren was allegedly killed.'

'Allegedly?' the disclosure stopped her dead in her tracks and him with her. 'What's allegedly about it? We've just attended his funeral, haven't we? We saw him cremated, didn't we?'

'Well-er, not exactly.'

'Not exactly? How exact does it have to be for you to consider him dead? We both saw his coffin.'

'I grant you if he'd been lying in it when it hit the flames, he'd have been burnt to a cinder. But the fact is, what we were privy to was no more than a facade. I told you who I thought the murderer was, didn't I, and you didn't believe me?'

'What of it?'

'You should have. I was proved right. The poor sod, the one with a bullet-hole in his body, is still stretched out on a slab in the morgue, and he never ever answered to the name of Warren. If you remember, after our dinner together, your father agreed to check on the body. He informed Buzz of his findings and was told to keep mum.'

'So that lets pop off the hook. But if you knew, Nat, what excuse have *you* got for keeping quiet?'

'I was also sworn to secrecy.'

She yanked her arm free and eyed him up and down. It made him feel nervous.

'We're partners, aren't we? And aren't partners supposed to trust each other?'

'Ye-es! And I trust *you* one hundred per cent. But I was given no choice. Apart from Buzz, General Halstenberg, Buzz's superior, insisted I should keep the matter under my hat. Believe me, I'd have given anything to confide in you.'

'You don't say!'

'I most definitely *do* say.'

But Erm wasn't prepared to give him the benefit of the doubt. 'How come *you* were let into the secret?'

'Buzz introduced me to the General the other day and I grabbed the opportunity to put my theory to the test regarding the identity of the murderer. The General instructed Buzz to phone your father. And that was that. Buzz thought the fewer in the know the better. He wanted to ensure that everyone behaved as natural as possible at the funeral. You *must* see that, Erm?'

Her set jaw suggested there was no must about it. And that meant the time had come to produce his ace card.

'If I hadn't been fully focused, partner, when coming out of Max's offices, the authorisation necessary to let you into the secret might well have escaped me.'

'Authorisation? But there hasn't been anyone around to authorise you?'

In an instant, her jaw eased out. Thankfully, from his experience as an accountant, a confused state of mind is never an aggressive one.

'And I think you ought to know, whilst I was concentrating on Max Goldbloom's reading of the will, I became aware of a definite inconsistency and I'm certain you'll agree we should investigate the matter at the earliest possible opportunity.'

'What inconsistency?'

He outlined the details and was relieved to see her brow returning to its normal smooth self.

'In future,' she told him, 'we don't keep secrets from each other and we pool *all* our knowledge, as and when. OK?'

And her OK was returned with an added smile. 'So what do you think has happened to Oliver?' asked Nat, 'and where do you think Warren's hiding out?'

'As the shock of discovering an alive and kicking Warren Tate has yet to sink in, I'll take a rain check on the latter, if you don't mind. But I'd like to sort out the Oliver Jupp mystery myself whilst I'm here in Fort Jackson.'

'But *you* just said we should pool *all* our knowledge?'

'And we will, partner. But until I've checked it out, I can't be sure. So as yet, it's not exactly knowledge.'

'I suppose so.' Though it wasn't what Nat really thought, it instilled in him the desire to produce a suitable quid pro quo. 'And whilst you're testing out your theory, I can do the same by testing out my theory as to Warren's present location.'

'And is your theory based on knowledge?'

'It's based on a gut feeling.'

'Nothing more than that?'

'Well, nothing much more than that.'

She let it pass. 'If this is to do with Hank and his connection with Saint Luke's, I'm not sure it's a wise move for you to go anywhere near the place. But as it won't take long for me to test out my theory regarding Oliver Jupp, I can join you later.'

Nat promised to keep in touch with her on his mobile. He told her he would aim for the wooded area around the monastery at the top of the Ridge. 'One thing you should know', said Nat, 'is that Buzz considers Warren a major National Security risk. "Effing traitor" is how he described him. Also, he believes other moles exist and need to be flushed out into the open.'

'That means you must tread carefully. Don't do anything to attract attention and don't take any unnecessary risks. In fact, don't take any risks at all.'

'You mean act like an ordinary chap, minding his own ordinary business, taking an ordinary constitutional in the woods. And whilst I'm about it, I shall look for a safe vantage point overlooking the Monastery, but only if it's at a safe distance from it.'

'You're not trying to be funny by any chance?'

'As if I would?'

'Don't make me laugh.'

'As if I could?'

'That you can! Like coming out with all that garbage about being fully focused and having the authority to tell me about Warren Tate. You've yet to discuss the matter with anyone.'

'That's not my fault, Erm. In accordance with Buzz's instructions, I was only too willing to put Spencer in the picture regarding the contents of the will as soon as I left the building, and it was up to him to pass the information on to Buzz. But it was also up to Spencer to give me the nod on Buzz's behalf in order to apprise you of Warren's return to the land of the living.'

'But you didn't tell Spencer a thing?'

'Yes, I did!'

'All you said was that Annie needed him.'

'So? Max read the will out to all of us including Annie.'

'But you must admit, you're more on the ball.'

'Just as well, as it happens. If you'd watched Spencer as closely as I did, you'd have observed the nod he gave me before he legged it.'

On the outskirts of Moose City, Big Rock Ridge rises above the town by almost 6,000 feet. Since the mid 1880s, Saint Luke's Monastery has stood on top of it as a monument not only to religious fervour but also to farming enterprise. With its large plateau situated just below the highest point of the ridge, the lower side displays a variation of jagged rocks interspersed with wispy under-shrubs and wild plants clinging on for dear life to crevices in the rocks. The face offers the brave (or the foolish) the chance to pit their climbing skills against the odds of plummeting down the sheer drop.

On the other and slightly higher side, the slope is much kinder to the would-be adventurer and varies from fairly steep at the summit to a gradual easing of the slope's gradient on its way down to the foot of the Ridge. The vegetation on that side of the Ridge is extensive and embraces a multitude of the wild flowering azalea intermixed with the deep-blue spikes of the lupin and the golden balsamroot set in between stretches of majestic ponderosa pines.

Before the creation of the present-day zigzagging macadam road, only a few tracks existed and most of those were difficult to negotiate. Up to the 1920s, the Order of Bearded Monks regularly carried on their backs, as well as on the back of their mule, all their produce and materials up the tortuous ascent from the trading post of Wapiti (the original site of Moose City) to the Monastery. Local records disclose the fact that at that time, the name given to their mule was Theo (a contraction from the Greek, Theodosius, meaning Gift of God). As far as the monks were concerned, Theo was a much loved and indeed a much appreciated gift, but only on the occasions where his willingness to assist overcame his natural stubbornness to remain in a static position when fully laden.

Usually Theo's willingness was coaxed via a steady supply of home grown carrots. The goods carried by the mule or by the monks were either purchased or bartered for in exchange for surplus produce, or in exchange for the monks' own carved and fashioned wooden utensils and chairs. These were carried down to the trading post in like manner.

The only part of the Ridge capable of being readily cultivated was on the plateau itself. To this day, the monks continue to farm its arable land, though over recent years various high, brick walls have been erected around the land as well as around the Monastery itself. Overall, the walls encircle an area of more than one and a half acres, including the Monastery's various outhouses, and a walled garden containing a variety of flowers and shrubs.

Some 6,000 feet or more below the Monastery, Nat was seated behind the wheel of his car. His adrenaline was flowing fast and from past experience it tended to urge him on to ever greater heights. Though in this particular instance, it was set on urging him on to ever greater speeds in order to obtain ever greater heights. He zoomed passed the late Hank Kepler's wooden verandered bungalow with hardly a glance at it or at any of the other similar looking homes dotted along the Ridge's lower slopes. He sped on upwards to negotiate the first of the hairpin bends, braked hard, swung the wheel up and down, and skidded around it. With no vehicle in sight, Nat made full use of the width of the road. But when a Cherokee Jeep appeared from out of nowhere heading towards him at speed, his automatic reaction was to close his eyes. From the screech of brakes that followed and with no resultant impact, he knew the Jeep must have swerved passed him. He blinked nervously in relief and decelerated to negotiate the next bend. For a moment, he felt a twinge of conscience. He glanced up at his rear-view mirror and he could see the other car skewed across the road. The twinge of conscience returned. He quickly blocked it out of his mind and continued on regardless. But the more he focused his thoughts on the investigation, the more pumped up he became and the more erratic his driving became.

He mulled over the fact that Erm was not only optimistic about locating the absent Oliver Jupp but reckoned it wouldn't take her much time to do so. Also, he felt sure that the connecting link between Hank and the monks was the key to solving the case and, according to Nat's understanding of the conversation he'd overheard between Hank and the monks huddled together in the park, a certain trip had been postponed. But why and where were they intending to go? He wondered who was likely to be included in the party and what the purpose of the journey might have been?

As he considered the various alternatives, mouthing a few words as he did so, all of a sudden his lips parted and the silence was broken.

'Good God!' he cried out. Didn't Hank refer to one of the monks in the park by name? He felt certain he had. But what was the name?

It was on the tip of his tongue, something beginning with Con. . .Constant? Finally, he got it and punched the air with glee.

'It was *Constantine*!' he screeched.

Feeling extra inspired, Nat focused on the next imponderable, being that of the ball game due to be held the next day between the home side and a bunch of suckers (according to Brad, Moose City's well known and well respected newspaper vendor). Brad bawled out to those within earshot that the bunch of suckers answered to a name reminiscent of a funfair's attraction, Dodgems. At least, that's what it sounded like to Nat. But as Brad spent his day calling out the news in an indecipherable manner, who could tell? Matters didn't improve much on a one-to-one basis either. Brad was almost as strident and just as incomprehensible.

If the monks' radio was still on the blink, it was likely, Nat argued to himself, they'd tune in again to the commentary on the ball game as close to the transmitter's beacon as possible. As the beacon was sited next to the park, another session in the park seemed definitely on the cards, providing, of course, no philanthropic busybody ruined the whole thing by donating the wherewithal to cover the cost of a new battery or whatever else was needed to get the radio's sonic waves up to scratch.

A parking area had been constructed at the highest point of the Ridge on the far side of the last Z-bend. At that point, the road levelled out for a few yards before dipping down to the Monastery's old, lofty, ornate gates.

Nat swung the wheel to the right and pressed his foot down hard on the brake. The car careered through the car park's narrow entrance, missing the posts on either side by a whisker. It skidded on beyond the specific area set aside for parking purposes and finally came to a halt on a flattish area in a tangled mass of bushes. A few more feet and it would have encountered the obliqueness of the hill's slope on the opposite side to the drop. Yet Nat put it down to his skilful driving. He'd steered the car through the entrance, negotiated a path through the trees, and avoided everything on the way.

He stayed put in the car for a while whilst toying with the idea of turning it round and delaying matters until after tomorrow's ball game. But as he was within striking distance of the Monastery, he convinced himself that all might be revealed once he'd had a chance to make contact with anyone within hearing distance of his soon-to-be-located vantage point overlooking the Monastery's grounds. And better still, if the monk contacted turned out to be Brother Constantine himself, his answers to a few leading questions could well wrap up a major part of the case.

But there were second thoughts. What if he puts his foot in it?

He gave it third thoughts and concluded that provided he proceeded with care, he couldn't go wrong.

He withdrew his mobile from the glove compartment and eyed the undergrowth through the car window with a degree of uncertainty. He tried the door. It opened a couple of inches. He applied more pressure and it shifted enough to thrust a leg out. He half stood up and pressed his weight against it. It capitulated in a flash. He landed on all fours in a clump of stinging nettles. The yell that followed was closely followed by a display of remarkable agility. He also managed to retrieve his mobile on the way up.

Inside the car park itself, the Cherokee Jeep drew to a halt. The driver stepped out, looking more than a trifle bewildered. On hearing Nat's cry of anguish, the bewildered expression changed to one of comprehension.

It prompted the removal of a Colt 2000 pistol from its holster.

With a click, the 15-round magazine was inserted and with no safety catch of its own, the gun was primed and ready for action.

The stalker edged forward, pointing the gun in the general direction of the cry.

The slamming of a car's door heralded Nat's imminent appearance.

The gun was raised and aimed at a gap in between the trees and a finger was curled around the trigger.

As Nat's eyes were set on finding the rough track leading up to the wooded area at the top of the Ridge, he failed to notice the stalker's presence, let alone the gun.

Cra-a-a-ck!

The bullet whistled passed his ear. It rooted him to the spot and sent a flock of birds skywards and Nat's mobile downwards. The bullet came to rest in a notice board displaying the word: DANGER!

As the crack of the pistol echoed down to the valley below, Erm was filled with trepidation. She was driving along near to the Big Rock Ridge intersection with an elbow resting nonchalantly out of the patrol car's window and a hand resting just as nonchalantly on the wheel. She'd changed back into uniform once her father spotted the cowgirl-style civvies she was wearing. He insisted on it, especially as she was driving one of *his* patrol cars and (as he put it) "not a horse in a wild-west rodeo show".

The reverberations of an exploding bullet made her sit up straight. She grasped the wheel firmly in both hands and pressed her foot down on the accelerator as hard as she could.

With one eye on the road and the other on her mobile, she prodded in Nat's mobile number. Her original intention was to phone him before leaving Fort Jackson, but after completing her mission concerning the absentee, Oliver Jupp, she was keen to see the look on Nat's face in person when relating her findings to him.

He didn't answer, though she knew his phone was turned on.

The car sped on up to the first corkscrew bend. At the bend she took a leaf out of Nat's book and skidded round the curves.

High above, the stalker moved forward. As best he could, Nat flung himself behind the large trunk of a tree.

Cra-a-a-ck!

The bullet ripped through the bark.

He scrambled back on to his feet and edged his head out a fraction in an attempt to identify his assailant.

Cra-a-a-ck!

He withdrew it, none the wiser. During that brief moment his head was stuck out, a flash of light blinded him. He imagined it was from the gun's discharge, but if that was the case, he wouldn't have survived to tell the tale. Later he realised it came from the sun's rays reflecting off the roof of the stalker's car, a split second's difference between life and death.

Step by step Nat retreated backwards, making sure that after each stride the trunk of the tree still continued to obscure the stalker's view. And once his heels touched the main track leading up to the wooded area at the top of the Ridge, he spun round and took off like a bat out of hell (or at least as fast as an overweight bat could make it). The track's numerous twists and turns kept Nat on the blind side of the stalker. But once inside the woods, the track straightened out and this left him with no alternative but to veer away and cut out a channel of his own through the trees.

He ran and ran until his legs began to turn to jelly. In desperation, he flung himself into the undergrowth.

Cra-a-a-ck!

The bullet whistled passed him, and it was by an unlucky quirk of fate that his dive was directed into another clump of stinging nettles. This time he stifled his natural reaction to leap up in the air and holler and swear, and he even had the presence of mind to hold a hand over his mouth to cover the sound of his gasps for air. His lungs felt as if they were about to explode and the pain from the constant stings of the nettles was excruciating. The latter forced him to edge forward into less unfriendly territory and whilst doing so, ease himself round enough to face his adversary.

Through the leaves, a pair of legs and a barrel of a gun crossed his line of vision. As the gun wasn't pointed in his direction, it lent credence to the most heartening notion to cross his mind since his ear felt the draught of the first shot. The owner of the legs was in the dark as to his exact location.

'I know you're somewhere nearby, Nat.'

He recognised the voice instantly and pressed his hand even harder over his mouth to stifle an exclamation of incredulity.

Of all people, it was Esther!

'Best to get it over and done with, don't you think? One shot is all it takes. Whereas if you keep on riling me as you did back there on the hill with your appalling driving, I could make it a hell of a lot worse, with each shot more agonising than the last.'

Esther moved one step at a time in the direction indicated by the barrel of the gun. She appeared to be heading for a clearing in the trees.

'Surely, you don't want that, do you, Nat? It's much better to pass into oblivion without feeling a thing. All you need to do is to give me a sign, a word, some movement, the snap of a twig. The slightest thing will do the trick.' Nat was relieved to see she was convinced he'd gone to ground in the vicinity of the clearing. 'It's nothing personal, you understand. You must believe me, Nat, when I say we like you. Truly, we do. Warren's often spoken highly of you both as a person and as his financial adviser, and we both reckoned you were just right for the part. I grant you, you're clever with figures, but apart from that, need I say more? No offence meant. But then *you* had to go and spoil it all. Went and nodded off when Warren was acting out his death scene. And after all the trouble he'd taken to set you up. You'd have hit the headlines, you know, a kind of celebrity. Ungrateful, is what I call it.' Nat watched her take another step forward and cock an ear. 'I guess you figured it out, didn't you? You wouldn't be here otherwise. Given time, Warren was convinced that even *you* could manage that.' A red-crested woodpecker swooped and rustled the leaves of a tree.

'I wonder if you figured out which one it was? Which one of them drew the short straw? Did you come up with the one that really *looked* the part, Brother Caleb? Not that it matters one way or the other. Dead men can't talk, especially when all that's left of one of them is a heap of ashes.' On the other side of the trees, the clearing extended over gnarled roots peeking through the ground between smooth layers of decomposed leaves and vegetation. 'How on earth was Warren to know his trip would be delayed at the last moment? By now, he expected to be far, far gone from here. What a pity it didn't go according to plan. A pity for you, that is. As it is, what can I say? Parting is such sweet sorrow. But when you've got to go, dear Nat, you've just got to go. There's no two ways about it.'

Low down on the tree, the woodpecker began to prod the bark with its beak.

Rat-a-tat-tat!

Cra-a-a-ck!

With a whoop of glee, Esther charged forward, but in the elation of the kill, failed to notice the protruding roots. Her feet came to an abrupt halt and slid backwards whilst her body was still intent on going forwards. The Colt 2000 flew through the air and landed not that far from the mangled remains of the woodpecker.

Nat could swear he heard a voice in the background. But he didn't hang around long enough to find out. He legged it through the undergrowth as fast as his legs could carry him back along the same route he'd cut out when fleeing in the opposite direction. On hitting the original track, and in the hope of attracting a monk's attention to his plight, he headed for the top of the Ridge. He concluded upwards was better than downwards. But it didn't take long for him to realise his mistake.

With a feeling of nausea rising up from the pit of his stomach, the reason for the danger sign in the car park had become only too apparent. A few yards into the section of the track overlooking the Monastery's grounds, it turned into a gaping hole. This was partially filled up with a number of rocks piled on top of each other covering about four yards of the would-be track. Unfortunately for him, the highest point of the rocks was near enough the same distance below his feet.

In horror, he turned to face Esther, but all he was staring at was the open space behind him. He couldn't make it out and in his confused state of mind, decided to risk everything by scampering back down the track heedless of anyone lying in wait for him along the way. He continued on unimpeded until he reached the comparative safety of the car park and an anxious-looking Erm.

Nat flung his arms around her and in between gasps for breath, spluttered incoherently into her ear.

'L-a-aw tr-tried to-to kill-ll-ll...'

'Take your time,' she said, 'and tell me nice and cool-like who it is who's trying to kill who and what the law has got to do with it?'

'*Not* law, Law-rence! Est-her Lawrence.'

'I guess you were right about her.'

'Except she was supposed to be working for Buzz. He's CIA, not FBI. But she's in with Warren. He's CIA, too, or at least he was until he...'

His voice tailed off as he focused his eyes beyond her at the car park itself. The only car he could see in it was her patrol car.

He staggered back unable to credit it and pointed a quivering finger in the direction of her car.

'Where on earth's it gone?'

Erm spun round instantly. 'Where on earth's what gone?'

'Her car? It must have passed you by on the way up.'

'Other than for the local bus, no vehicle came down the hill as I was driving up it.'

'But if that's the case, Esther must have turned right instead of left out of the car park and parked her car either inside the Monastery's grounds or on this side of its gates.'

'And what about your car? Has it gone missing, too?'

'Of course not! I parked it out of sight for safety reasons.'

'So it wasn't your car that caused all those skid marks?'

'I'd hardly call them skid marks.'

'And what would you call them?'

'I anticipated the uneven surface when driving in between the trees and braked accordingly.'

'You amaze me, partner, you sure do. I know you have a way with words. Sometimes it comes out like gobbledegook, but then, as likely as not, it turns out to be anything but, other than for the recent exception.'

'What-do-you mean by gobbledegook?'

'You said you *parked* the car. I reckon if it hadn't skidded to a halt where it did, you could have finished up in a tangled mass of metal somewhere between here and the bottom of the Ridge.'

'That's not fair! You knew where it was all along.' He eyed her reproachfully. 'In any case, it's not gobbledegook. It's spin! And I was in a hurry.'

'But not in as great a hurry as Esther.'

'Huh?'

'You say Esther's been trying to kill you. As her car's gone and you were put out not to find it here, she must have beaten you to it. But I get the distinct impression she was the one doing the chasing and not you.'

'I can assure you, she was right behind me.'

'But in the end, she was way out in front of you.'

'I saw her slip over on the ground and took the opportunity to make a dash for it. She could have caught me up as easy as pie, especially as I went the wrong way, up instead of down the hill. That must be how she got ahead of me. On the other hand, why didn't she hang around to finish me off?'

'I guess she must have got cold feet.'

'But it doesn't make sense.'

'Any more than it makes sense not ringing for help or answering my call.'

'When the bullet whistled passed my ear, I dropped the phone and couldn't risk recovering it.' As he spoke, he walked towards the signpost and scanned the ground around his feet. 'And guess what? Here it is...' he bent over to pick it up. 'As good as new.'

'It sure is your lucky day, partner, in more ways than one.'

'Maybe it is, but Esther must have seen me drop it. And it was clearly visible, too. So why didn't she pick it up on her way back to the car? She could have prevented me from calling for help.'

'Maybe she didn't think of it.'

'As a vindictive psychopath with a gun in her hand, I'm certain it'd be one of the second things to come to mind.'

'What's the first?'

'To pump a bullet into one of my vital organs.'

'The first thing that comes to my mind is to phone pop and fill him in.'

'And whilst you're at it, tell him about Brother Caleb as well. He's the one stretched out on a slab in the morgue.'

'How d'you know for sure?'

'Esther kept rabbiting on to me in the hopes I'd break cover or reveal myself in some way. In so doing, she was good enough to provide me with the necessary corroborative evidence.'

'Bully for her! Is that the guy in the photo we saw at Hank's place, the one who's the spitting image of Warren?'

'Looking like two peas in a younger Warren and Caleb's pod.'

'What d'you reckon? Where's Esther disappeared to and why?'

'Why is even more difficult to calculate than where. And where could be anywhere on the bus route.'

'It's the first time I've heard of anyone making a getaway by bus.' She prodded the buttons on her phone. 'Let's see what pop thinks.'

She spoke for only a few minutes.

'Pop says to give him a ring as soon as we've located the car.'

'It's nice to know he's got such faith in us. It's best if we make use of Shank's pony. Less conspicuous, don't you think?'

Erm agreed... 'It's a matter of keeping ourselves, and especially my uniform, hidden from view as much as we can. If I walk real close to where the branches and undergrowth stick out over the verge, it should offer some measure of cover.'

They carried on in silence down the hill until they were almost within touching distance of the Monastery's main gates. But there were no signs of a car parked on either side of the road, and if Warren was inside the Monastery in the guise of Brother Caleb, they couldn't risk alerting him to their presence by attempting to enter the grounds.

They sat down on the grass to assess the situation.

'I heard the sound of gunshot near the bottom of the ridge,' Erm opened up, 'and for sure everyone else must have heard it, too. So as you legged it, you reckon Esther had company?'

'Yes! And what if it was Warren? He's bound to have told her to put a lid on things as she was attracting attention.'

'So she gives up the chase, though she knows you know too

much for your own good, and more to the point for *their* own good, and dumps her car some place in order to catch the bus. Or alternatively, she seeks refuge in the Monastery, with or without her car.'

'The more I think about it, Erm, the less I like it.'

'You're right! I just can't buy it, the bus or the Monastery. The Monastery's much too near for comfort; it could blow Warren's cover. The bus is too slow, and any place the bus can go, a car can go too. So why take the bus?'

Erm pulled herself up on to her feet and pulled Nat up to join her. She told him about her findings as far as Oliver Jupp was concerned, and after she'd finished, they both felt more dejected than ever.

'As far as I can see,' said Nat, 'it's back to the bloody drawing board.'

With hands clasped together, the couple entered the travel agents and were greeted by a male member of staff beaming at them from behind his desk.

'Do. . . do please take a seat,' he gushed, 'and how can we be of service?'

The couple sat down, still holding hands.

'Well,' said the man, 'we are anxious to select the holiday of our dreams and pick the most idyllic place on Earth for our . . .' he hesitated before lowering his voice, 'for our honeymoon.'

'May I on behalf of "A to Zee Vacations" wish you both long life and much happiness together, starting with many, many days of leisure in some distant part of the globe, in some part that's warm and sunny, in some part that's always inviting, in some part that will be remembered and treasured by you both for the rest of your lives,' he held up a brochure for inspection. 'How about Honolulu?'

The girl shook her head. Her companion squeezed her hand and nodded in agreement.

'We were looking for something...' he said, 'something different. Some place, perhaps, a little less warm and a little less sunny. We were wondering what you have on offer in Siberia?'

'Siberia?' the travel agent wobbled on his stool.

The girl offered an explanation. 'We're both terr-i-bly interested in wild plants and all that kind of stuff.'

The travel agent gulped noisily.

The man made an effort to elaborate on his fiancee's explanation.

'We particularly like studying them in their natural surroundings. *Nepeta nuda* and *Aquilegia glandulosa.* That sort of thing, you know.'

The travel agent admitted that he didn't know.

'I'm not sure what we have on Siberia. Maybe you could suggest which part of it you had in mind?'

'What do you think, Jonquil?'

'*Jonquil*?' she gave her fiancé a less than loving look.

'Would somewhere like Khabarovsk be of interest? We could get you there by way of the Trans-Siberian Railway, and from there you could go even further, if you like?'

'Thinking on, I'd like to go further, Bartholomew.'

'*Bartholomew*?' The look he gave her was also less than loving.

'Yeah, Bartholomew! I'd like to go further. The further the better.'

'And does my Jonquil prefer to go by plane or by train?'

'Plane, Bartholomew, out of good ol' Khab-whatsit.'

Bartholomew turned to face the member of staff again. 'What airlines operate out of Khabarovsk? Have you a list by any chance?'

The travel agent's computer failed to elicit the required information. This resulted in a fair amount of manual delving until a list was found. But first Khabarovsk had to be located on it. After that, the travel agent was able to make reference to various airlines and their various destinations. When he reached one particular airline, Koryo Air, Bartholomew rose abruptly from his seat and unceremoniously yanked his companion up with him.

'You've been most helpful, hasn't he, Jonquil?'

'Indeed-dee-do, he has, Bartholomew.'

'We'll have to give it much thought,' said Bartholomew as they headed for the door.

'Please do!' the travel agent regained his guff. 'We can book any of those airlines mentioned to any of the destinations mentioned, anytime, other than for the last one.'

At the door they turned once more to face the travel agent. 'Thank you. We're much obliged. But one has to get it right for a honeymoon.'

The travel agent agreed.

'I and my bride-to-be will spend some while mulling it over, though at the back of my mind I can't help feeling . . .' he looked at his bride-to-be for support, 'I can't help feeling Honolulu might prove to be the better choice.' Jonquil nodded her head up and down with vigour.

Chapter Sixteen

The chug-chug of a helicopter's rotor blades reverberated through the air. Sheriff Kramer raised his eyes and glared.

'You wouldn't know it but the choppers supposed to be acting discreet-like, not hanging around like a king-sized hornet about to stick its sting in. Look at it, Connor, damned turbulence everywhere? It's ruining the flow of me locks,' he made a vain attempt to flatten the hairs edging his bald pate. 'What kind of idiot do you think is flying the thing?'

'I guess it could be Buzz,' suggested Connor.

'Although he may fit the description to a tee and he is the guy responsible for the idiot up there, I can tell you for sure, whoever it is, it ain't Buzz.'

'Maybe Buzz hasn't told him what to do?'

'Who knows? So far, he hasn't told me what to do, either. And what he has told me hasn't exactly boosted my morale or filled me with enthusiasm. It's like dealing with a dumb-cluck without the cluck. It seems his left hand is trying hard to keep his right hand in the dark. Typical CIA.'

'Nahr, Oswald. If he's CIA, his right hand's bound to know what his left hand's doing.'

'Wanna bet?'

'Anyhow, I thought he was FBI.'

'As far as you're concerned, Connor, he *is* FBI. As far as I'm concerned he's CIA. You see, I've been sworn to secrecy. My lips are sealed,' he gave him a sly wink.

'I don't get it?'

'You're not supposed to get it, Connor. I'm not supposed to get it, either. Today for-instance, when a softly-softly approach is called for, *he* goes in with all guns blazing. But getting back to the pilot of the chopper, it sure ain't Buzz, chiefly 'cos if you care to look behind you, you'll see his car's parked on the other side of the road. When I last saw him, he was kind of smouldering. As a matter of fact, what I told him seemed to upset him no end. Can't think why? Now he's in urgent need of a word with Erm and her partner.'

'Her partner?'

'That's what she calls Nat. She says it's purely professional, but Siobhan and I reckon there's more to it than that. If they can catch the killer or put him out of action, with or without our help, it's on the cards their partnership will blossom in every direction. And Nat's raring to have a go.'

'But he ain't the kind of guy to tackle a killer.'

'Nahr! Tackling paperwork in an office is about his mark. Still, he's got some bright ideas. In fact, he came up with one of 'em recently concerning the case and talked me into going along with it. I promised to give him and Erm time to check things out and let them have the honour of disclosing their findings to Buzz in person afterwards.'

'What did they want to check out?'

'The likely route and destination of our number one suspect.'

'Who's our number one suspect, Oswald?'

'Warren Tate.'

'But ain't he dead?'

'Until I checked on the body myself, I was also fooled into thinking that way. The Doc was in on it, you see, and the initial evidence backed him up by suggesting that Warren was shot whilst Annie and Bennett were in a position to witness the shooting. In fact, the murder took place about half an hour earlier. That's when Warren's stand in was shot dead in Warren's boat. Traces found in it matched his DNA.'

'Do we know whose body it is?'

'The unlucky guy was a Saint Luke's monk called Caleb.'

'But didn't ballistics reckon the rifle was only fired once?'

'It was! More than one shot would have given the game away. The second shot was meant to fool us and probably came from the killer's handgun.'

'But you said Warren was our number one suspect?'

'He is! But we've got more than one killer on the loose. I bet Warren cursed his luck when he couldn't spot Nat standing on the opposite side of the lake. Maybe he and the gunman arranged some kind of signal as to when to press the trigger. If so, it didn't work. Warren was facing Annie and Bennett and not the gunman, as Caleb was forced to do when the initial fatal shot was fired. That made it even harder to credit that it was Nat who fired the shot. And the bank account opened up in his name didn't ring true, either. I reckon it was meant to add weight to the concocted evidence by giving the impression he was also getting money on the side. Blackmail, maybe? And Warren made sure the source could be traced. He wanted us to find out, though he should have made it a touch less obvious. If extraction is the name of game, whoever pays the piper sure doesn't want the tune to be played. But at least Warren was clever enough to choose a day to act out his murder when I wasn't around to check on things, including the body. Warren knew he couldn't fool me but he also knew it wouldn't take much to pull the wool over Annie's eyes. The Doc said it was Warren. Both she and Bennett knew they'd seen Warren standing on the jetty, so who else could it be? And whatever they used to bind and gag the victim left only the barest of marks on the arms and hands and around the mouth. But I can't say I blame you or Elmer for not spotting the real thing. Though I admit you *did* spot the patchy look of the face. Once the beard was shaved off, that's how a weathered face would look. All the same, I'd have been on to Warren a darn-sight sooner, if you hadn't failed to pass on the message from the gardener.'

'But I took down the details, as I'm s'posed to do, and Elmer put it on file.'

'Yeah, under Hardy. How was I to know that? I haven't time to read every darn file. I should have been told.'

'Look?' Connor pointed skywards. 'The chopper's moved off.'

'You're not trying to change the subject by any chance?'

'Of course not, Oswald.'

Further along the road, the helicopter was once again in hovering mode.

Erm was sheltering with Nat low down by the side of her patrol car in an effort to reduce the effects of the dust storm swirling above them.

'So this is where you've been hiding?'

The scowl on Nat's face was mirrored by the one ridged across Erm's brow. They rose in unison to square up to their accuser.
'We're not hiding, Buzz,' Erm let rip. 'We're trying to avoid the stupid antics of your chopper.'

Buzz reacted by swivelling round on his heels and extending a hand upwards. Purposefully, he twisted it to and fro in the air. And the response was instant. The helicopter rose, turned at an acute angle, and sped away.

'He was waiting on my instructions,' Buzz sounded almost apologetic. 'However, I gather from the Sheriff that you, Nat, have been helping my fellow agent, Esther Lawrence to improve her target practice. Apart from your incredible luck in managing to survive the experience, as a result of your intermeddling, the lady has gone to ground. Hence, the necessity to comb the area in order to locate her and her co-conspirator, Warren Tate, who I reckon has gone to ground with her. You have completely ruined our ruse regarding Warren's funeral and have put us to a great deal of trouble and expense, including the services of a good many men and cars, plus the cost of a chopper.'

'But. . . but . . .' Nat attempted to offer an explanation but was waved into silence. In any case, Buzz hardly drew breath.

'I would point out that this most senseless display of bravado on your part was recounted to me by the Sheriff and not, as I would have hoped, by yourself personally, being the one responsible for originating the present sorry state of affairs,' Nat made another futile attempt to tell his side of the story. 'Clearly, it's not just you, Nat, who's acted irresponsibly. Erm failed to follow her instructions to operate *only* in a liaison role. I commend enterprise as and when circumstances dictate. Necessity is the mother of invention. As long as mother remembers that it's father who lays down the law.'

Whilst Erm struggled to retain her composure, Nat hoped she would allow him to get his word in first. He told her it might help her to appreciate Buzz's position.

'After all,' he said, 'even though he's the man in charge of the case, he has a superior breathing down his neck, and I'm certain you'll agree that we must avoid treading on Buzz's toes at all costs. We must allow him to report what we have to say to the General first,' Erm began to look upbeat. 'In my opinion, Buzz,' Nat started off, 'the consequences of my "intermeddling", as you call it, are not as detrimental as you suppose. And may I stress that I wouldn't have left it to the Sheriff to put you in the picture had I not felt it necessary to turn what was no more than a hunch into something of substance. I do not regret my actions. To be honest, I feel quite proud of them.'

'How can you feel any pride,' Buzz screeched, 'at the mess you've landed us in?'

'With respect, it is not of my making. I gather Spencer's in charge of the on-the-ground operations and I imagine Esther and her car are bound to fall into your lap sooner rather than later. In my humble opinion, widening the search is more likely to alert Warren to the fact that you're on to him than anything I may have done.'

'You...you...' spluttered Buzz indignantly, 'you have the gall to switch the blame away from yourself and on to *me*? And what about you two, may I ask? Earlier on, two kids were playing in an area specifically set aside for recreational activities at the top of the Ridge and one of them accidentally struck their ball into the bushes. It bounced right back at them off what their parents later discovered to be the boot of a car, Esther's car, to be exact. How did you manage to miss it? Didn't either of you notice the Family Area next to the car park?'

'Of course we noticed it,' said Nat, tongue in cheek. 'Unfortunately we didn't have time to check it out. The Sheriff contacted you about Esther and you instructed him to instruct us to return to Moose City.'

'You also told pop that time was the essence,' Erm chipped in.

'And what's that got to do with it?'

'It dictated our course of action.'

'Action, Erm! What damn action? You were ordered back to base.'

'And we did return. We hardly spent any time at all verifying Tate's current location, and Nat was literally counting the minutes as he prised out of Brother Constantine sufficient info to point to Tate's future plans.'

'Are you trying to take the piss?'

Erm shook her head and fought hard to keep her expression as blank as possible. Nat came to her rescue by assuring Buzz that what he was suggesting couldn't be further from the truth. He told Buzz that apart from a telephone call, the digression they made on the way back was the clincher. He felt certain Buzz would agree.

'We'll see about that...unless by chance,' Buzz laughed jeeringly, 'you've managed to solve the case.'

'We wouldn't go as far as to say that,' Nat beamed back at him, 'but we have come up with the answers to a few leading questions,' Buzz's face was a mixture of incredulity and exasperation. Nevertheless he contained himself and invited Nat to elaborate further. 'Brother Constantine,' Nat continued, 'was one of the monks in the park with Hank on the day he was murdered, and I can also assure you that from the way Esther behaved in the woods, neither she nor Warren have yet to cotton-on to your ruse. She's convinced that the monk was cremated in Warren's place.'

'And d'you happen to know his name?'

'I certainly do! He was, and still is as far as Warren's concerned, a monk by the name of Caleb. And having seen an old photograph of him clean-shaven, his resemblance to Warren is remarkable. And it was Warren, as Caleb, I observed standing in the shadows of the trees in the park whilst Hank and the others were huddled over the radio. Apparently, his back was giving him gyp and he couldn't bend it to listen in with the others. As it was Hank who acted as the Monastery's barber, one can appreciate Warren's dilemma. Close up, his false beard would have stood out a mile. And Hank was set to trim the monks' hair and beards the following day. The poor sod never even saw the light of it. Also, a special trip is on the agenda for some of the monks, and it's one that Warren's intent on joining. Unfortunately for him, but most fortunately for you Buzz, there's been a last minute hitch. Had everything gone as planned, Warren would have been out of the country by now and you wouldn't have had a hope in hell of catching him. As it is, you'll find him in the Monastery, acting the part of a man of the cloth and, we can but pray, hating every minute of it.'

Buzz's interest in Nat's story suddenly took on a new dimension. He moved out of earshot, produced his mobile, and as far as they could tell, was in the process of issuing fresh instructions. Once he'd completed the call, he returned to face them again.

'Maybe you had a lucky break, Nat, and things went your way. But you should bear in mind that this Constantine monk could be stringing you along,' though his words rang hollow when he added, 'and what else did he tell you?'

'It was mostly about the monks' proposed trip. You see, I couldn't understand why it'd failed to get a mention in the local rag. After all it was news of a sort, and at first I thought I must have missed it when browsing through the paper. But as my browsing tends to be fairly in depth, I began to think the monks might be bent on avoiding publicity. But why should they want to do that, I asked myself? It bugged me to such an extent, I felt compelled to throw caution to the wind and telephoned Brother Constantine himself for an explanation.'

'You did *what*?' Buzz let rip. 'You could have blown it big time.'

'Could have, but I didn't. When I spoke to Constantine, he was about to make the coffee for his farming brothers. I told him I was Hank's friend and was in the park on the day he died. I extended to him and his fellow monks my sincere condolences. And believe it or not, it did the trick. He opened up more and more. It seems that the Abbot himself, Justin B. Hepplewhite, supervises all farming activities. His main disciples are Caleb and Constantine, plus a couple of others, but their passionate sideline is botany and horticulture and as a separate group they planned to join a larger group of their Saint Luke's Brothers in order to attend a special religious and pacifistic event overseas. First, the smaller group would depart on their own to experience the joys, as Brother Constantine put it, of viewing and recording details of the flora within a region of the world noted for the rarity and variety of its plant life. After that, they would rejoin the others for the main attraction. Unfortunately, the effects of a stomach bug rendered the Abbot temporarily incommunicado and forced a hurried rearrangement of their itinerary. This meant that for the smaller group of monks, the last and only religious stop of the tour would become the first and only religious stop of the tour. I imagine Warren would have been literally spitting blood at the delay and at the prospect of having to attend a Multi-Religious Service of Commemoration on the epicentre of the 1945 atomic blast in Nagasaki's Peace Park.'

'Warren's heading for Japan? That can't be right.'

'I'm certain it wasn't part of *his* original plans. But don't you think such a visit should have warranted at least a mention in the local press?' As Buzz opened his mouth to express an opinion, Nat closed it again by giving him a taste of his own medicine. Nat kept going. 'I put the question to Brother Constantine and was told that the Abbot had thought it best not to publicise it. As numbers were limited, it might upset those unlucky Brothers who were forced to stay behind. But I can't help feeling that to find out afterwards might be even more upsetting. According to Brother Constantine, those attending the event were chosen arbitrarily, though I very much doubt that such a choice applied to the smaller group of monks. Luckily, Constantine saw no reason to keep it to himself. After all, as a professional man and one of Hank's friends, he knew he could rely on my discretion.'

'Wants his head examining.' For the first time since they met, a semblance of a smile touched Buzz's lips.

'What makes you think that?'

'To rely on *your* discretion? Blabbermouth!'

Nat gave him a withering glance. 'Unlike the Abbot, I don't intend to hush things up.'

'You reckon that's what he's doing?'

'In my opinion, the Abbot's reticence is due in no small part to the fact that he's arranged to spend almost half of his allotted time engaged in a pursuit on what seems to me to be nothing more than a form of pastime. And what's more, they'll be doing it miles away from the main party of monks. If I were a cynic, I'd be inclined to believe that the overall outlay was coming out of ecclesiastical funds. Also, I'd be equally inclined to believe that the Abbot was not a follower of baseball. Although he is able to raise sufficient funds to go half way round the world and back, he seems loath to raise sufficient funds to cover the measly cost of resurrecting a particular radio. But be that as it may, the separate jaunt arranged for the select band of monks is intended to embrace such floral delights - Brother Constantine's words, not mine - as *Bergenia crassifolia* and *Gentiana altaica*, to name but a few.'

'What kind of plants are they?'

'To be honest, I haven't a clue. But Brother Constantine was so pumped up about them, he repeated the names over and over again.'

'And whereabouts in the world does one hope to find those kind of plants?'

'In Southern Siberia.'

'But that can't be right, either?'

'At first, it didn't sound right to us,' said Erm. 'But after paying a visit to "A to Zee Vacations", all was revealed and Bartholomew came up trumps.'

'Who?'

'It's a guy I met at the travel agents.'

'Don't you mean, "we met"?'

'Oh, no!' said Nat. 'Erm met Bartholomew, whilst I had the pleasure of meeting the girl of my dreams. The one I intend to marry. She answers to the name of Jonquil.'

Buzz looked baffled.

'But what about Erm?'

'What about her?' said Erm. 'If Nat wants to marry Jonquil, I reckon it's fine by me. And for my part, I'll be happy to tie the knot with Bartholomew.'

Nat beamed his approval.

'You mean, neither of you care a tinker's cuss about the other? Gees! I'll give "A to Zee Vacations" a wide berth in future. *My* partner isn't that easy going.'

'But they were such a mine of information,' Nat told him. ' "A to Zee" advised us of the direct flights operating between Khabarovsk in Southern Siberia and Niigata airport in Japan. More importantly, Khabarovsk is one of the few airports in the world where the national airline, Koryo Air, operates with direct flights to and from P'yongyang in...'

' . . . North Korea.' Buzz interjected.

'That's what we came up with,' said Erm.

'Trouble is, Warren was into our top secret Gemini trials and North Korea could be but a staging post for onward despatch to a major power, one that's doing business with us and where neither us nor them would want to rock the boat.'

'Have you a country in mind?' asked Nat.

'In mind, yes! And there it will stay.'

'D'you think Warren could jeopardise your work?' Erm inquired.

'Very much so. With his phenomenal memory, who knows what he can conjure up from out of the back of his mind? And who knows what we can conjure up to help turn his turning to our advantage?'

'What's with the memory and the turning, Buzz?' Erm was keen to know more and for once he was keen to tell.

'Warren is one of those guys blessed with a photographic memory. In the past, it's been a great asset to us, but now it could be our Achilles heel. And as for turning, there are always ways and means of turning a disaster into a triumph, like the leaking of false information, for example. Do it right and the rewards are plenty. The question is has Warren passed on information concerning Gemini? Whilst he's still around, we reckon it's all in the mind . . . *his* mind. But what we need to do is to flush him out into the open. And in a perfect world, we should do it in such a way as to get him on his own.'

'And in a imperfect one?' Nat asked.

'If we could figure out when and where Warren's likely to be outside the Monastery at any set time, that'll be as perfect as we can expect.'

'We can help you out on that one, Buzz,' said Erm, nodding her head at Nat as she spoke. In response, he opened up the palms of his hands invitingly.

'There's another ball game due to start soon and we reckon that within the next three hours you should be able to locate your quarry in City Park somewhere near the place where the monks met on the day Hank was killed.'

'How d'you figure that one out?'

'Apart from being look-alikes, the only thing Warren Tate seems to have had in common with the monk, Caleb, is his love of baseball.'

'Warren used to attend every home fixture without fail,' Nat advised him, 'and chances are he'll be in attendance today, though on this occasion not in person at the ground.'

'But, instead,' said Erm, 'with Caleb's usual buddies, now that Hank's no longer around. With him out of the way, Warren can join in with the rest of them, listening in to the commentary on the monks' radio.'

Slowly and deliberately, Buzz shook his head.

'No-no-no! According to your way of thinking, the venue for tackling Warren or not in City Park rests entirely upon the need to renew the battery of their radio. A mite tenuous, wouldn't you say? And what happens if someone's provided them with one?'

Nat reckoned there was little chance of that.

'Constantine made it clear they were planning to visit City Park for their usual listening-in and intend to board the bus to Moose City, giving them sufficient time to walk from the Bus Depot to the park with about half an hour to spare.'

Erm was quick to point out that the local timetable should show the time of the bus they're likely to catch.

'That's all very well, Erm, but there's no guarantee Warren will be on it?'

They rated it a fair certainty.

'Why not let Spencer check it out?' suggested Erm.

'But he's otherwise engaged.'

'You mean he's still searching for Esther? And I'm sure he'll find her, once he looks in the right place.'

'And where, may I ask, do you think that is?'

'You just told us where her car was found. Why should Esther go to the trouble of hiding it? If she wanted to make a getaway, a car's the obvious choice. Also, why didn't she finish Nat off when she had the chance? He agrees it would have been dead easy.'

Nat shuddered visibly. 'A little less of the dead, if you don't mind, partner.'

'Also,' Erm went on, 'how could she have known in advance that Nat would take the wrong turning? Otherwise he wouldn't have finished up behind her. Answer: Somebody else moved the car. It's the only thing that adds up. So who moved it? And what happened to Esther? As the sound of gunshot could have attracted attention, how d'you think Warren Tate would have reacted to that?'

In Buzz's opinion: 'He sure would have seen red.'

'Red enough to kill?'

'That depends on how he rates her. You see. Warren wasn't making phone calls from his boat on the lake. He was receiving them, and that explains Esther's role. She was feeding him with Gemini data. I should know, I've been feeding it to her for some while, though mostly of the inaccurate kind. But until recently, we weren't sure as to the identity of the one she was passing it on to. And whereas his conquests came naturally, he's been trained to kill. So where he thinks his own survival's on the line, I reckon the latter is more likely to take precedence over the former.'

'Then you might as well call off the cavalry and let Spencer and his men go native in the woods, maybe as a bunch of walkers exercising their legs around the area where Nat last saw Esther.'

Erm was amazed to see how Buzz accepted her advice without question.

Once more, he moved out of earshot before producing his mobile. Within a few minutes he returned with the phone still clutched in his hand. He told them that one of Spencer's men would be positioned overlooking the bus stop near the Monastery's gates. Buzz wanted to know the minute the bus departed, though he sounded far from convinced that Warren would board it.

'Oh, ye of little faith.' Nat chided him.

'Faith I have in abundance. It's facts I'm short on. And that leads me to our initial essential fact which you, Nat, are about to supply to Spencer.'

'Eh?'

Buzz handed him the phone.

'He'll need to know the exact route you took from the car park to the place where you and Esther parted company.'

By the time Nat finished giving Spencer directions, the other two were clicking their heels impatiently.

'You didn't miss anything out, did you?' said Erm, with a touch of irony.

'Like what exactly?'

'Like how many separate twists and turns are there in the track for Spencer and his men to follow?'

'I wasn't that long on the phone, was I?'

She heaved a sigh. 'At least it gave me time to think.'

'Me, too,' echoed Buzz. 'I was thinking as to how we could isolate Warren from the other monks in the park?'

'I was thinking,' said Erm, 'that if Warren Tate reckons he's fooled us into believing he's a monk, why can't a few of your men also fool him into believing they're monks too?'

'What're you driving at?'

'If some of your men were dressed up as monks, it might be possible for them to replace the genuine ones in the park, or at least as many of them as possible. I reckon it could help to give you the edge.'

'But you're assuming I can get hold of a supply of authentic-looking false beards and rig-outs in less than three hours.'

'Maybe you can.'

'How?'

'As it happens, Fort Jackson has one of those fancy costumiers. It's called "Gorgeous Garbs and Winsome Wigs" and they supply costumes and wigs for stage shows, parties and the like. Only last week the local theatre staged a musical on one of Nat's old English kings, the one who had a queen with a French sounding name and more than his fair share of knights. There were guys in it dressed up like monks, all pious and po-faced, whilst the knights downed the local beer and sang and danced around a round table with the local village hookers. And they wore beards, too.'

'The hookers?'

'No, stupid! Monks.'

'Did you see the show, Erm?' asked Nat.

'Nahr! It's not my scene. But I read about it and had a good look at the posters outside the theatre when I went by.'

But Buzz was seething with rage. 'Who-are-you calling stupid?'

Without batting an eyelid, Erm replied, 'From the pictures on the posters, the monks sure looked stupid to me.'

Buzz eyed her with suspicion.

'And Buzz could put his chopper to good use as well,' said Nat, enthused by his partner's suggestion. 'It's about the only thing that'll get him to the costumiers and back in time, and his men would have a golden opportunity to switch places with the genuine monks when the genuine ones are in need of a visit to the khazi for a quick slash.'

'Khazi?' Buzz raised his eyebrows.

'A comfort station,' Erm informed him.

'A quick slash?'

Erm raised her eyebrows at Nat.

'In a hurry to relieve the bladder.'

Suddenly, Buzz, too, was in a hurry to go, though where, he didn't say.

But what he did say was: 'What I can't understand, Nat, is what made Esther get so damned worked up as to want to take pot-shots at you in the first place? She's noted for being calm and collected and in control of herself at all times. For her to do that, suggests she lost her cool in a big way.'

'I can't be certain, but I put it down to the modern day scourge that erupts from out of some motorists' subconscious minds, including the minds of the most normally even-tempered of people, into an uncontrollable mass of "whatever it takes, I'll get the bugger" type of aggression, and from my personal experience, it does it for hardly any reason and does it every time.'

'Every time?' questioned Buzz.

'Road rage! Drivers are quite unreasonable nowadays.'

'You reckon so?'

'Granted, I was deep in thought at the time and she might have had to put her brakes on rather sharpish. But we didn't collide, that's the main thing, and she did manage to skid to a halt further down the hill.'

'I assume Esther passed you on your way up to the top of the ridge.'

'A car was coming down the hill as I was going up it. It seems likely she was the driver of a Cherokee Jeep.'

'Likely? Don't you know?'

'My eyes were closed at the time.'

'Based on Nat's own admission, Erm,' said Buzz, wagging a finger at her, 'I reckon you could do him,' he straightened the finger and pointed it at Nat, 'for dangerous driving. Though you may need to obtain corroboratory evidence from the driver of the jeep. Lucky for Nat, that might prove to be insurmountable.'

'I don't look on her disappearance as my good fortune,' Nat growled back at him.

Buzz's smile was much more evident. He told them how well they'd gone up in his estimation and that he would personally let the Sheriff know it. In fact, he thought Erm was ideally suited for a special assignment he had in mind. She was to act as a warden (and the Sheriff and his men were to follow her example) once the trap had been set in the park.

Erm inquired as to what he meant by "warden" and was advised that whilst Buzz and his men were otherwise engaged in putting Warren out of action, she and the Sheriff and his men would be helping to keep the members of the public out of his hair. He called it "a vital contribution towards the solving of the case".

But once Buzz was out of earshot, Erm opened up with a vengeance. It appeared that Buzz's head was too big, his eyes were too close together, his mouth spouted shit, and his ears had nothing in between. And he was "a worthy member of the Corps of Illegitimate Assholes".

'Fancy that!' Nat sounded astonished. 'One can't blame them for only using initials.'

His words brought a smile back to Erm's face.

Nat suggested they should move off before Buzz could instruct the Sheriff in his new duties and before the Sheriff had time to pass on his instructions to her.

'Why not change out of uniform at home and park your patrol car at Fortuna? We can make use of my car instead. Let's aim for the woods at the top of the ridge and with any luck you'll be the one to discover Esther's body up there.'

'But what do I tell Spencer if we meet?'

'Tell him to keep his mouth shut.'

They got in the car and she grabbed the wheel, did a three-point turn, and headed in the opposite direction to where she knew Buzz and her father would be having their tete-a-tete.

'Pop may not like it when he discovers we've hit the road.'

'He'll like it, once he knows the score. And with any luck, us hitting the road will make Buzz hit the roof.'

'I must be mad to go along with you. What happens if Spencer beats me to it?'

'He won't.'

'How can you be so sure when you've given him such detailed directions?'

'Detailed they may be. Accurate they're not.'

'What are you saying?'

'I'm saying I've been a bit economical with the facts.'

'I have to hand it to you, partner, you never cease to amaze. Guess that's why I like you so much.'

'Only like? Back there, I got the distinct impression we'd become engaged?'

'In uniform, it's like. Out of it, it's love.'

Nat closed his eyes. 'I'm getting the picture,' he smirked.

'But what about Spencer?'

'Let him find his own woman.'

'I mean, being sent on a wild goose chase.'

'You can't call it that, Erm. I'd say it's more of a mystery tour. Walking is good exercise . . . so everyone keeps on telling me.'

'Trouble is I've got a kind of sickly feeling deep down inside that my suspicions are about to be realised.'

'What suspicions?'

'By going along with you, even if my screw's loosened up a turn or two, I suspect your screw's hanging by a thread.'

'My dear partner, all it is, is a touch of nerves. May I suggest a swig of brandy to help you relax or a finger or two of your father's rye whiskey might do the trick. Alternatively, should all else fail, I'd recommend a good screwdriver.'

'Nahr! I can't abide brandy or rye, or any of them fancy cocktails either.'

Chapter Seventeen

Burr-burr...burr-burr! As the phone's plastic sounding warble filled the air, Annie's grip on her book tightened. She was on the verge of discovering the identity of Jonquil's secret lover and the phone had picked the wrong point of time to gain her attention.

Burr-burr...burr-burr!

She strove for all her worth to blot out the sound.

Kirk seemed the obvious choice, she thought. Tall, dark, handsome *and* unattached. But Perry, tall, fair and rugged husband of the promiscuous Jodi was also a good bet. But what about Bartholomew, she mused? He may be a touch on the short side and a trifle overweight but he did have a certain indefinable quality, even though no one seemed able to define it. In addition, it'd been emphasised over and over again the depths of his warmth, though noticeably not of sufficient depths to raise the inner temperature of his cold bitch of a wife, the flat-busted Melissa. And he could be on the lookout for someone a touch warmer (Jonquil was noted for her friendly disposition) as well as someone a little less flat-busted. Jonquil did fit the bill, as clearly demonstrated in the tennis match with her coach, Robert Thingummybob, when the coach nosedived from four-love up in the set to a four-six loss after the net tore and Jonquil gamely removed her bra and stretched it across the gap.

But finally, the phone's incessant drone won.

She lifted it up, wrapped her fingers around it, and squeezed, wishing she could throttle it.

'What d'you want? Whatever it is, I'm not buying. And if it's anything else, you've got ten seconds, starting from...'

The voice on the other end of the phone ignored her opening gambit and responded with an animated: 'Hi-i-i, babe!'

As if by magic, her face was transformed into wreaths of smiles. In an instant, the book and its characters (and their various relationships) were consigned to the back of her mind.

'Hi, Spencer! How's tricks?'

The phone's constant ringing had brought Bennett to the other side of the half open study door. He was set to enter the room but on hearing Annie's voice, hesitated and cocked an ear instead.

Spencer was quick to inform Annie of Esther Lawrence's disappearance. He told her that it was likely she'd found herself a new boyfriend and in the course of time would emerge once more into the light of day.

'Do you mean that nice and helpful insurance girl?' she said.

'Yeah, Annie,' he winced at the description, 'that's the one I mean.'

He went on to relate his main reason for ringing. He'd be free shortly and would like to call on her to discuss "something of a personal nature", the details of which he felt were necessary to impart on a one-to-one basis. She was highly delighted. Conversely, Bennett was anything but. He stomped off along the hallway tentatively trying the handles of the doors in the hopes of finding an empathetic spirit ensconced behind one of them.

In the dining room he was greeted with a request to "take a powder" if his intention was to hang around for any length of time depressing everyone with his long face. This was coupled with the advice that the most beneficial powder he could take (after he'd taken a powder) was one to ease his apparent guts-ache. Alternatively, if what was bugging him was emotional rather than medical, he should let "the world" know and perhaps "the world" could help some? "The world" was all ears. On hearing this, Bennett opened up,

Meanwhile, Annie was also feeling in need of an empathetic spirit. She bemoaned her current lot into Spencer's all-attentive ear by making repeated reference to the shabby way she'd been treated by Warren, especially as to the way he left the bulk of everything he possessed to his wife "of all people".

Spencer did his best to smooth her ruffled feathers and recommended she should try to fill her mind with higher things, like "man and woman together as one with hearts reaching out in search of true love" and all that jazz. His words had the desired effect as she filled her mind with the possibilities and probabilities as to the identity of Jonquil's secret lover. She suggested that it would be nice of him if he could delay his arrival by several minutes to allow her time to read on and get all the low-down.

He assured her that it'd take him longer than several minutes to get to her, and added: 'Who-the-heck's Jonquil?'

She spent the next ten minutes providing him with a résumé of the storyline, finishing up with the list of candidates, Kirk, Perry and Bartholomew. He was too flummoxed to consider the matter in detail but promised to give it a great deal of thought whilst on his way down to her.

She informed him: 'It'll be a test of our true love.'

Spencer's hopes soared and the hand holding his mobile developed a tremor.

'You-mean, Annie babe, if I can pick out the name of this Jonquil broad's lover, we can become an item?'

'Maybe! But irrespective as to which one it is in the book, I want to find out if you and I are on the same wavelength. Man and woman together as one with hearts reaching out in search of true love.'

'And all that jazz,' added Spencer.

'Yes! That as well.'

'Trouble is, Annie, by the time I get to you, you'll know who it is.'

'True! But I promise to write down who I think it is as soon as I put the phone down. And that means it won't matter one iota who it turns out to be in the book.'

'But what happens if I get it wrong?'

'How can you possibly get it wrong, Spencer? Believe me, if we're truly suited, deep down inside you'll *know* instinctively who it is. If you like, you could write down the name as well. That way, you won't have to give it another thought until we meet. Just relax and carry on with whatever you're supposed to be doing.'

But as he didn't have a clue as to the name, he knew that carrying on with whatever he was supposed to be doing was going to prove difficult. And to relax wasn't even a remote possibility.

Chapter Eighteen

'Well?' Erm tapped her foot on the ground impatiently.

'Dodgy!'

Once again the track divided into two.

'I'm of the opinion, I'm sorry to say, that as a direct result of the appalling circumstances surrounding my enforced gallop up the slope, my natural powers of observation have been adversely affected. At the time, my mind was not so much concentrating on the vagrancies of the course underfoot but more on ensuring that as much of a hindrance as possible lay between me and that ghastly trigger-happy woman. I find it most unfortunate.'

'And how d'you think *I* feel? It's *most* unfortunate you gave Spencer the wrong directions over the phone. Judging by the trouble you're having trying to remember the right ones, the wrong ones might turn out to be the more accurate of the two.'

'You're being sarcastic again.'

'Can you blame me?'

'I can tell you, partner, it's a bit off-putting when I'm trying to direct all my mental endeavours into formulating an in depth assessment of our current situation in order to pinpoint the pros and cons arising therefrom.'

'You're trying to do *what*?'

'I'm trying to think.'

'*Trying*? There's a word that springs to mind.'

He extended a finger in the direction of one of the tracks. 'I'm certain that I would have kept to the track likely to give me the best chance of survival. Although they both disappear round a bend, the one on the right disappears out of sight several yards before the one on the left. I suggest we plump for the one on the right.'

'But in *your* state of mind, you could have taken either route?'

'But the one on the right looks familiar.'

'Why didn't you say that in the first place?'

As they continued on up the slope, it didn't take long for Nat's natural trudge to deteriorate into a snail's pace. And Erm felt obliged to lend a hand. She went ahead of him and placed her hand behind her back, inviting him to grab hold of it. Noticeably, his pace increased as she helped pull him along, at least that is until Nat spotted a particular opening in the trees, whereupon he wrenched his hand free and left her searching frantically for something to hold on to. She landed flat on her face. But he was oblivious to her plight. His eyes were fixed unwaveringly on a flattened swathe of vegetation, one he had flattened out himself on his previous visit. As he lolloped along the same route, he emitted sounds of jubilation.

Erm, on the other hand, emitted sounds of a different sort and in a manner that seemed to belie the existence of any partnership between them, professional or loving. The pitch of her voice was sufficient to ensure it carried far enough to offer a glimmer of hope to a fed up and frustrated Spencer. Almost at once he recognised Erm's dulcet tones. The descriptiveness of her language intermixed with Nat's name proved to be the clincher. As she set off in hot pursuit of Nat, Spencer (and his men) set off in the direction of her voice.

The effort she put into catching him up helped dissipate the heat bubbling up inside her, and by the time she reached him, her anti-feelings had mostly turned into rivulets of perspiration, though a feeling of pique still remained.

He was standing motionless by an overhanging tree next to a large clump of stinging nettles, his high spirits deflated like a burst balloon. Erm was ready to give him a mouthful but one glance at his mournful face was enough to change her mind.

'What's up, Nat?'

'Oh, 'tis cruel the twists and turns of fate.'

'Having grazed my hands, knees, and suffered a hurt pride, I'm not sure I'd go so far as to call it cruel. Damned unthinking, that's for sure.'

Nat eyed her up and down with concern. 'You haven't fallen over by any chance?' he asked, in all innocence. 'I noticed the track back there was very uneven and if I hadn't felt so elated at discovering where we were, I'd have held back to give you a helping hand.'

'I didn't, and don't, need a helping hand, thank you very much. It's you that needed one. Remember?'

'Come off it, Erm. You were the one that fell over.'

'You...you...'

'Cast your eyes down there?' He directed a finger at the nettles. 'Can you see the outline of a pair of shoes through the leaves?'

'You . . . you . . . you mean, Esther's down there?'

'Looks like it, and of all things, Warren hid her body in those awful stingers. Oh, 'tis cruel.'

'Cruel! How can it be cruel? Esther wouldn't have felt a thing. Only the living feel pain and I guarantee the living can feel it in all kinds of ways on the outside as well as on the inside.' She dropped down on to her knees and peered into the undergrowth. 'I could do with one of your handkerchiefs, preferably one that's clean.'

He produced a handkerchief with a flourish and assured her it had yet to touch his nose or any other wipeable part of his body. And it was large enough to protect both hands.

She gingerly extended them under the shoes and grasped the heels firmly. She flexed her muscles and pulled hard. Whilst the shoes flew through the air towards the underside of a branch of the overhanging tree, Erm finished up flat on her back, and at the angle the shoes struck the branch, the return trajectory was set to pass through Nat himself. As a result, he suffered a double thwack to the head.

Any thought of making humour out of the situation vanished in a flash. He rubbed the targeted area ruefully and stared down into the mass of nettles. Staring right back up at him through the leaves were the sock covered soles of a pair of feet. From their position, he could see the owner was stretched out face downwards and not upwards in keeping with the shoes.

Erm gazed up at him with a reflective look on her face as she moved herself into a more comfortable position.

'The ground isn't as hard as you'd think,' she informed him. 'It's kind of spongy-like and easy on the ass.'

'Well, I can tell you, Erm, those shoes weren't the least bit spongy-like or easy on my bonce.'

'Can you see them?' The shoes had come to rest near a tree. 'For Pete's sake, don't pick 'em up, will you?'

'Why ever not?'

'Use your head.'

'I just did, didn't I?'

'In that case, without looking, tell me what kind of shoes they are?'

'I suppose you're going to tell me they came from some classy footwear boutique?'

'No! I'm going to tell you they're elasticated. And though we know Hank's glasses hit the deck when Warren Tate yanked him off his feet, *his* shoes stayed put, yet he'd been kicking out like mad. That's 'cos *his* shoes were laced-up. If Warren killed Esther the same way as he killed Hank, she'd have struggled and kicked out likewise. Her shoes would have gone the same way as Hank's glasses.'

'That means Warren must have picked them up and slung them into the clump of nettles *after* he'd dumped the body.'

'And that means..?'

'The nettles could be a blessing in disguise. If you hadn't made use of my hanky, you'd have smudged Warren's fingerprints for certain. As it is . . .?'

She bounded back up on to her feet and tickled him under the chin. 'Who's a clever dick?'

'The way things have been going recently, I'm convinced it can't be me.'

'Why are Brits so modest?'

'As a nation we suffer from a superiority complex. Naturally, we do our best to hide it as much as possible by letting the other chap beat us at most things.'

'You *are* pulling my leg?'

'If only? But perhaps we'd best concentrate our minds on pulling Esther's legs, and her, out of those damn nettles.'

Erm tore the hanky in half and Nat wrapped his half around his right hand whilst Erm wrapped her half around her left hand. Once suitably protected, they bent their knees and backs and extended their hands through the leaves enough for each of them to grab an ankle.

It only took a few reverse steps for the body to be dragged clear.

They slung their half-handkerchiefs to one side and Nat stepped over the body next to Erm in a position to turn it face upwards. Together, they thrust their lower arms beneath it and heaved. It rolled over with comparative ease but left the head sideways on.

They both gasped in horror.

Nat gulped nervously but was determined to save Erm from any further distress. After all, Esther and Erm had been true-blue buddies and although, he reflected, Erm seemed to be masking her grief remarkably well, Esther's demise must have hit her hard.

He placed a leg on either side of the body and bent over to grasp the back of the head. As it wobbled disconcertingly in his hands, the colour of his cheeks drained away and his palms oozed sweat. He wiped them a few times across his trousers and was thankful for the existence of the trees. They were blotting out the sun, making the air around his head feel cool and refreshing. It steadied his nerves. But he wasn't prepared for the sight in store.

He'd witnessed Hank's eyes bulging out of their sockets but this was much, much worse. The face itself was distorted beyond all recognition. Esther's beauty in life was transformed into extreme ugliness in death. Nat stumbled back, mesmerised by the sight. An acrid taste filled his mouth as he let out a belch. His stomach was telling him to look the other way but his mind was unwilling to register the advice. He belched some more, and it took the sound of a voice, like an echo resounding inside his head, for the spell to be broken.

'That Tate guy's got a hell of a lot to answer for.' They both shot round to face the speaker. 'As you have, too, Nat, I hasten to add.'

'*Spencer!*' The name exploded inside Nat's mouth.

'Yeah! At least you've managed to get that one right. About the only thing you've got right since we've been wandering around these woods in ever increasing circles. We've covered an enormous area, including pastures new where I reckon no man has ever set foot before. Now *do* correct me if I'm wrong, Nat . . .'

'I can explain.'

' Have you any idea what it feels like to be sent on mission impossible by someone you thought was a responsible kind of a guy, someone you thought you could trust, someone you thought wouldn't play games?'

'The main thing is we've found Esther.'

'And at my expense, I see.'

'No, I wouldn't say that. Erm will tell you, won't you, Erm?'

'Yeah! He's right there, Spencer. It was at my expense as well.'

'Take no notice of her. She's feeling a bit sore. We couldn't remember which way to go to start with and when we did, Erm tripped over in the excitement.'

'It was *you* who made me fall and it was *you* who couldn't remember the way.'

'I wonder why that doesn't surprise me?' Spencer observed. He moved to take a closer look at the body.

'Can't you cover the poor bitch up?' Erm suggested. 'It's giving us the creeps.'

Nat's eyes opened wide in amazement. Wanting the body to be covered up was a sign of respect. Referring to her as a bitch, poor or otherwise, was not. Erm must be really stressed out, he thought. Mind you (he gazed at her long and hard) she didn't look stressed out one little bit.

'My men will do the necessary.' Spencer bawled out his instructions.

'And that reminds me the shoes need to be bagged up with care,' Erm told him. 'Tate's dabs are likely to be on 'em.'

'All part of the service.'

He issued further instructions, including one covering the removal of the body.

'And that reminds me, what exactly *are* you doing here, Erm? The last thing I heard was that you and your father were due to take up special duties in City Park.'

'Special duties, my ass! Acting as one of Buzz's lapdogs more like it.'

'Buzz says it's all in a good cause.'

'Oh, yeah! Do I look like a lapdog to you?'

'Not from where I'm standing.'

'So *you* can't have seen one, can you? And you should bear in mind, Nat doesn't mind taking the rap for this one.'

'Hang-on-a-mo?'

'Well it was your idea, partner. Remember? In any case, Buzz can't touch you. You're a civilian as well as a foreigner.'

'In England, civilians are the ones who get arrested.'

'You don't have to worry about that. You're not an American citizen, so Buzz will have to be doubly sure. Even then, he won't arrest you. If the worst came to the worst, he'll get pop to do it for him.'

'And that's supposed to make me feel better?'

'But you won't have to take the rap if Spencer's willing to forgive and forget and agrees to turn a blind eye.'

'I thought..?'

'It never pays to think, Nat,' Spencer was quick to advise him, 'especially when dealing with those of the opposite sex. Up to now, I never knew I was as blind as a bat, but I guess I must be.'

Nat tapped the side of his nose meaningfully. 'You mean your lips are sealed?'

'So you reckon I'm dumb as well as blind?'

'No-no, not at all. May I offer you my sincere thanks and a promise to return the favour as and when required.'

'As a matter of fact, as and when could be right now. Maybe you and Erm can help ease my mind.'

'How?' Erm asked.

'Is Annie in on it or not?'

'In on what?'

'In on the fatalities. She identified the Caleb monk as the Tate guy, didn't she? She should have known it wasn't him. After all, she saw him at Fortuna day in, day out. How could she have made such a stupid mistake?'

Nat stared at him as if *he* was the one being stupid. 'If you really put your thinking cap on, Spencer, you should know the answer to that. You've had first-hand experience of Annie's natural tendency to turn on the waterworks or pass out at the sight of blood. Do you really think she's capable of murder or even assisting in it?'

'I guess she's a mite too highly strung for that.'

'A mite is putting it mildly. She thought she'd witnessed her uncle being shot dead. The sight on its own would have snapped her highly strung strings in a trice. And although the binoculars from the Rolls enabled her to identify Warren on the jetty, the most essential piece of equipment from Warren's point of view - and the real reason why he encouraged Annie to make use of his pride and joy Rolls - was the fact that it contained a built-in phone.'

'Hard to understand how an intelligent girl like Annie could ever fancy a guy like Bennett.'

'They say love is blind,' said Erm.

'Love? How can you even think such a thing, let alone say it? Anybody could see it wasn't love. He took advantage of her trusting nature and manipulated her into believing he was likeable.'

Erm was about to expand upon the matter when one of Spencer's men intervened.

Esther and her shoes had been bagged. The remains of the bird had been bagged. A cartridge case found nearby had been bagged. And they were ready to leave.

Spencer's men were to take the lead in single file with the coffin and pallbearers - a euphemism for the body bag and the men carrying it - screened front and back. Erm was to follow on immediately behind them, with Nat behind her. And Spencer would bring up the rear.

To any casual observer, the cortege must have looked somewhat strange as it weaved its way through the trees.

'But why d'you think a built-in phone was that essential?' Spencer put the point to Nat on their way down the hill.

'It's all to do with the manipulation of the evidence by the late Chester Cornell. We believe the doctor's task was to keep everybody at bay, other than for Annie and the police, and to ensure that no one was in a position to cast doubts as to who it was lying stretched out on the jetty. It also meant making sure those in the house stayed put in the house before the event and were either in the house or kept at a safe distance away from the body after the event. As Annie and Bennett, Oliver, and myself were absent from the house, on the face of it, there were only two residents for the doctor to worry about, Rosie and Amelia. I gather that the doctor dropped in initially to see Warren for a chat - and we now know what that meant - but as Rosie was feeling under the weather, he put on his professional hat and saw her as well. I remember Rosie telling me how her head was "throbbing fit to burst". The doctor diagnosed a form of migraine and prescribed some pills. He recommended a period of rest with the bedroom curtains drawn. In Amelia's presence, Warren asked the doctor to stay behind and await his return, though he knew the wait would be forever. He instructed Amelia to supply the doctor with coffee and any edibles he fancied. So when Warren left the house, he was supposedly intent on going on one of his fishing trips. Naturally, once he'd departed, the doctor was conveniently placed to intercept the phone call due to be made by the couple, Annie and Bennett, set up to raise the alarm. I was also set up as a witness, in more ways than one, though the doctor wasn't relying on me to make the call. Esther made that crystal clear. My role was to carry the can and Warren relied on me to witness his "murder". Previously, he'd told me to cut myself off from the outside world in order to appreciate Mother Nature uninterrupted. He made certain that I left my mobile behind and couldn't raise the alarm. I would have looked less likely to be the murderer, if I had, and he calculated how I would react, no doubt thinking I'd return to the house post-haste. Had I done so, I'd have become the number one suspect sure as eggs are eggs.'

'You were lucky,' Spencer remarked.

'On the other hand, without a phone readily available to Annie and Bennett, the doctor, and Warren, could easily have come unstuck, leaving Bennett with no option but to drive back to the house in order to raise the alarm. If that happened, there was no way of knowing who would get to the body first. You can see how impossible that would have been for the doctor. Also, there were no buildings in the vicinity of the lake likely to house a phone. In any case, it was a fair certainty Annie wouldn't have been willing to waste precious time searching for one beyond the parameters of the car. She could have taken her mobile with her, but Warren couldn't bank on it and for him to suggest any such thing was likely to raise questions then *and* afterwards. As it happens, Annie left her mobile behind. Apart from anything else, she'd have been hopping about like a cat on a hot tin roof, urging Bennett to drive back to the house flat out after he'd made that important phone call.'

The cortege eventually drew to a halt beside a covered van screened by various bushes. Once the body and other bagged items were placed inside it, the men and the van departed.

After a phone call, Spencer was told to hang on and await the return of the man posted as lookout. He was concealed strategically above the monastery grounds and was still awaiting the arrival of the bus.

'By the lousy way he treated Annie,' said Spencer, 'I'm looking forward to giving this Tate guy a good hiding.'

'And for Esther's sake,' Erm raised her fist demonstratively, 'I suggest a taste of woman power should be added to a good hiding. It'd show that women have the balls and he hasn't, not after I've kicked the living daylights out of 'em.'

The two men flinched in unison.

'At least it tells us one thing,' said Nat. 'You and Esther were indeed true-blue buddies.'

'What are you talking about? It proves nothing of the kind. Don't you guys know anything about women? If a couple of girls make out they're true-blue buddies, it's a sure-fire sign they can't stand the sight of each other.' The two men gaped at her in disbelief. 'The fact that I couldn't stand the sight of her alive, doesn't mean a thing now she's dead. No one - but no one - could stand the sight of her dead. And this time, it's not down to her but down to him. Any man who treats a lady like that deserves to be taught the lesson of a lifetime.'

'I agree!' said Nat. 'But before you both get carried away, think about Warren's main accomplice, the one who shot and killed the monk, Caleb, in order to create a stand-in corpse for Warren. The same one who I believe shot and killed Craig, the security guard, in an attempt to incriminate me after the original attempt failed, and the same one who killed the doctor, Chester Cornell, by knifing him over and over again. Whoever it is, it's someone who's quite ruthless, particularly callous, and equally as dangerous as Warren himself. Someone at Fortuna, perhaps?'

'But what can *I* do about it? We've got the Tate guy to sort out first.'

'You can do a great deal about it by getting on the phone to Annie.'

'Nat's right, Spencer. All that's needed is a touch of hocus-pocus. If you're willing to tell a little grey lie, with any luck you'll keep the accomplice, and Warren Tate, relaxed and happy in the knowledge that they've fooled us.'

'What's a little grey lie, Erm?'

'It's not a white one, that's for sure.'

Spencer again produced his mobile. She set out the details. The call seemed to go on ad infinitum. Afterwards, Spencer's face was a mixture of joy and misery. Erm complained of a crick in the neck due to her many attempts to overhear the conversation, and Nat complained of being shushed every time he opened his mouth. Erm urged Spencer to tell all.

'You'll never guess?' he said. 'Annie's set me a test to see if I'm in tune with her. Just as well she doesn't know I'm tone deaf. She *knows* I fancy her. But she still insists. Trouble is she's reading some senti-damn-mental book and wants me to work out who's the secret lover of one of the broads in it going under the name of Jonquil.'

At that point, Spencer's phone burst into life. The lookout informed him that the bus had arrived and that a number of monks were boarding it.

'All system's go!' Spencer whooped, as he charged off to where he'd parked his car. 'I'll wait for my man, Bart, in the car and follow you on down.'

'Isn't Bart short for Bartholomew?' Nat called out after him.

'We only know him as Bart. Bartholomew was one of the names in Annie's book, with Kirk and Perry. They were the main candidates for the part of Jonquil's secret lover. But who in their right mind would think up names like that? I mean to say, other than in a book, where in the world would you hear names like Jonquil and Bartholomew banded about?'

'In a Travel Agents?'

'In a *what*, Erm?'

'As a matter of fact, I rather like Bartholomew,' she yelled out at Spencer's disappearing figure.

'And I rather like Jonquil,' shouted Nat.

Spencer stopped in his tracks and turned round to face them again.

'In my book . . .' he cupped his hands round his mouth, 'you're a pair well matched. You're both half-crazy.'

They raised their voices as one to tell him how much they liked the sound of his book though they were quick to point out that they never did anything by halves.

Chapter Nineteen

It was a glorious sunny afternoon and the City Park was a blaze of colour. The normally unoccupied bandstand situated in the middle of it was playing host to a lively brass band. Stirring Sousa marches filled the air and the gentle breeze was wafting the music to all corners of the park. The band plus the warm weather had attracted a larger number of visitors than usual and the Sheriff's attempt to divert the public elsewhere was proving nigh impossible.

To make matters worse, the monks who'd alighted from the bus were nowhere to be seen. Those who were seen turned out to be the look-alikes acting under Buzz's instructions. They were promptly withdrawn from circulation until the whereabouts of the genuine ones were known. To rub salt in the wound the place in the park where they were supposed to gather had yet to record the presence of a single monk.

Buzz's men spotted Nat in the vicinity of the bus depot and instructed him to "get the hell out of it". He was quick to point out that as a civilian, he'd the right to board a bus or check the timetables. As regards Erm's whereabouts, Nat fancied she was somewhere about and was told in no uncertain manner to tell her to take up her duties in the park forthwith. Nat was happy to pass on the message, should he "happen to bump into her".

He did what they said, and he got the hell out of it. One minute he was arguing the toss with Buzz's men and the next he'd legged it to who knows where. But again, they failed to spot Erm, who had legged it with him. As soon as Buzz realised that Erm was still up to her prevaricating ways, he questioned the Sheriff as to his daughter's present whereabouts and found him vague and suspiciously indifferent. Buzz could hardly contain himself. It fell to Spencer to undertake a search for Erm and it didn't take long for him to find her; and Nat at the same time. Like many others , the two were seated on a bench in the park admiring the view and enjoying the musical accompaniment.

Erm was decked out in a turquoise-coloured blouse and skirt recently acquired from a local boutique. It was a two-piece that just about held the curves of her body in place. Upon seeing her ensemble, Nat inquired as to how she was going to house her gun, her mobile *and* her handcuffs, without them sticking out like three sore thumbs. She assured him that nothing was going to stick out as she'd bought herself a matching handbag to prevent such an eventuality. Nat passed on that one. But he did warn her that it might take longer for her to produce the gun from out of a handbag, should the need arise, and as it was Erm herself who'd insisted on them looking as inconspicuous as possible, he couldn't help but feel sceptical as to her own ability to blend into the background when every time they passed a male over the age of about twelve, the male's eyeballs shot out of their sockets.

Spencer was quick to remind them of his supreme sacrifice in misleading Annie and letting her down, (would she ever forgive him?) so he reckoned they should keep their minds on the job in hand. They assured him their minds were on the job in hand, not that that raised his spirits noticeably.

'Please take a seat?' Nat waved Spencer into a spare space beside him. 'You're getting all het up over nothing.'

'All I can say is you'd better have a good excuse, otherwise the way things are with Buzz, he'll have the two of you boiled in oil and barbecued for good measure.'

'If you must know,' Erm told him, 'we're waiting for Brother Constantine to appear. Or to be exact, we're waiting for him to reappear.'

'You've already met him?'

'Sure have! As Nat and Warren Tate know each other only too well, we thought it best if Nat took a back seat and I took up the advanced position in the bus depot. I got as near as I could to the monks to hear what they were saying but then, before I knew it, they'd disappeared into the depot's comfort station. Luckily, I caught sight of them trooping out again via the back exit. With the exception of Constantine, they all made a beeline for the footbridge over the Big Rock River. I waved at Nat to come on. At the time, he was being sidetracked by some of Buzz's men. They seemed to be giving him a mouthful, and it sidetracked them as well, thank goodness. There was no time at all to consider which monk or monks to tail. As Nat and Constantine had acted on the phone like a couple of buddies, we opted to tag along behind him.'

'Why didn't you put Buzz in the picture?'

Erm stared at him aghast.

'Buzz isn't exactly *my* buzzword, and in any case, I didn't have time, the Constantine monk strode along at a fair lick and I didn't want to lose him. I sure didn't want to lose Nat behind me, either.'

'Sounds like a tricky situation.'

'You can say that again! Keeping them both in view was getting more and more difficult by the second. But when I realised the monk was heading for Sam's Stall, it gave Nat time to catch up at the corner overlooking the stall. Sam sells hot dogs, hot and cold drinks and all that kind of stuff. He's right outside the park's main gates and we couldn't believe our eyes when we saw the monk ordering hot dogs and cans of soft drink.'

'And,' Nat added, 'whilst we were in the course of rubbing our eyes to see if we were wide awake or not, who should appear out of the blue but the Sheriff himself. He woke us up good and proper. Erm did her best to quieten him down by placing a finger across her lips and shoving him purposefully out of Brother Constantine's range of vision.

Whereupon, she spent a while explaining why we were where we were and in the process assisted the affable side of his nature to re-emerge into the light of day. The thought of us getting one over on Buzz seemed to fill the Sheriff with a certain *je ne sais quoi*. His buoyant mood increased to an even greater extent when after we'd discussed matters of interest with the monk, relating to his new found wealth, the whereabouts of his fellow monks, their dodgy radio and the pending ball game, Erm was able to inform her father of the outcome.'

'And what was that, may I ask?'

'Don't ask, Spencer.'

'Don't ask?'

'Even if I told you, you'd scarcely believe it.'

'*If*? There's no damned if in it. I want to know, Nat, and I'll let you know later if I believe it or not.'

'The fact is, Spencer, it was all down to Brother Caleb and as luck would have it,' Nat savoured the moment, 'he came unstuck.'

'Caleb, the Tate guy? How come he came unstuck?'

'It was, as you put it, the Tate guy. And the good news is that things didn't work out as he probably thought they would. Constantine told us that one of Caleb's relatives had donated a new battery for their radio, together with a generous amount of readies to cover a constant supply of refreshments throughout the entire course of the game. Sadly for Mr Tate, the snake of misfortune reared its ugly head and stuck its forked tongue out at him. It turned out that the culprit wasn't the perishing battery but the blinking radio itself. Apparently, it was on its last transistorised legs. I wouldn't mind betting the monks were only too aware of the situation, but since none of them was willing to raise even the cost of a battery, they preferred to lay the blame for the radio's inadequacies squarely but unfairly on the battery's shoulders. The generosity of the said relative knew no bounds. When he - Constantine referred to the relative as "he" - was told about the turn of events, lo and behold he conjured up a brand new portable radio like a rabbit out of a hat. And it came from a relative whose very existence, up until then, had been for the rest of them but a blank chapter in Caleb's book of life. Bearing in mind his fellow monks considered Caleb to be "frugal in giving", a euphemism, I suspect for being tight-fisted, he unwittingly put his finger on the nub of it all by saying, and I quote, "It's as if our dear brother was another person", unquote. And one can't say fairer than that.'

'But what I don't understand,' said Spencer, 'is why the Tate guy didn't listen in to the commentary with those like-minded monks *inside* the monastery? The Tate guy must have given them the radio to help reduce the risk of discovery by having to leave the monastery unnecessarily on the day before he's due to quit the US in exchange for a hero's welcome from a non-democratic state...a state that's known to be light on the welcoming side. More than likely, he'll be a gullible tool in their hands. I bet he gave the Constantine monk guy the dollar bills to go out and buy the refreshments well in advance of the game.'

'Except for the gullible tool bit, I imagine you're correct as to Warren's aspirations. Nevertheless, no matter how much safer he thought he'd be inside the monastery, he should have left well alone. The effect of his actions was to arouse the monks' suspicions and to increase rather than reduce the risk of discovery. In the past, the monks (including Caleb) looked forward to their regular trips to the park irrespective of their desire to listen in to the local ball game, and today was no exception. Due to Caleb's relative's generosity, they could listen in without straining a back or an ear in order to hear what was going on. But with Warren - as

Caleb - putting his oar in, the motion in favour of the usual venue in the park was no longer carried unanimously.'

'The Tate guy objected?'

'Too true he did. The minority against the motion was made up of Brother Caleb all on his lonesome. In my opinion, it was a complete lack of judgment on his part. Without realising it, he was acting out of character...the character of Caleb the monk. Warren may well have been able to copy his looks, his voice, and his general mannerisms, but when it came to his personality; he was very much out on a limb.'

'Maybe so, but where *are* the monks?'

'There was a change of plan. As soon as they arrived, they could hear the band oompahing away in the distance and as their regular haunt was in line with the path leading to the bandstand, they concluded that the band's constant beat would be too much of a distraction. Instead, they opted for one of the hides constructed around the park's inlet lake on the other side of the river and built for ornithologists and the like. There they hoped to follow the commentary without anything or anyone disturbing them and without them disturbing any member of the public.'

'But doesn't this monk guy run the risk of missing part of the commentary on the ball game? I reckon it'd have been far better for you two to do something more positive than just hanging around waiting for him to show.'

If looks could kill, Spencer would have been struck dead on the spot.

'And there we were thinking,' said Erm, with extra venom in her voice, 'that to pinpoint Warren Tate's exact location *was* doing something really positive. And another thing, the ball game isn't scheduled to start for another twenty minutes.'

'I suppose you're relying on the Constantine monk to do the

pinpointing.'

'You suppose correctly,' Nat informed him frostily.

'It's odd, isn't it?'

'What's odd?' asked Erm.

'Why neither of you even raised as much as an eyebrow as to how I managed to pinpoint your current location in the first place, bearing in mind the seat your asses are spread out over is but one of dozens of identical seats dotted around the park?'

Erm shrugged her shoulders indifferently. 'I guess you were lucky.'

'I assure you that luck had nothing to do with it. But I do have a nose for these things, especially when it smells a rat or rats.'

Erm gave him an old-fashioned look. 'And I'm beginning to get the feeling you know something we don't.'

'Wrong! All I know is what you two know already.'

'And that is?'

He pointed a finger at his chest. 'I know what you've been up to.'

Erm pulled a face at Nat. 'Maybe, it's time we came clean.'

'Just as there was no *if* about it, there's no maybe about it, either. Fact is, not long before Buzz instructed me to track you down, I received an interesting kind of a phone call, one that opened up my eyes to the deviousness of my fellow man and woman, and one of each in particular. As you know only too well, the Sheriff and his men are at present on duty in and around the park. That being the case, Buzz decided in his absolute wisdom to arrange for all phone calls to the Sheriff's office to be diverted elsewhere. I was given the task of dealing with the calls. Buzz reckoned the arrangement would thwart any attempt by the Sheriff, or any of his men or *woman*, to shoulder arms. Though I can appreciate how your father felt about having to do what he had to do, I reckon it was nothing compared to how I felt about having to do what I had to do. Handling calls to rescue "Fluffikins" stuck up a tree isn't my idea of crime-busting work. But to get back to the interesting phone call, it came from a man who was willing to disclose the fact that he was a local monk, but for some strange reason was unwilling to disclose his identity. Also, what was equally strange was his keenness to assure me as to how well he could keep his mouth shut. Too damned well, as far as *I* was concerned. Though he did let out he'd recently had the pleasure of meeting my Chief. To start with, I thought he meant Buzz. But when he called him "charming", I began to have my doubts, and the monk guy had his doubts too. He reckoned my Chief looked so young and attractive, it was hard to credit *she* was running the investigation. I agreed. It *was* hard to credit, but I didn't let on. He told me to inform my Chief that he would contact her at a certain bench in the park. This one, as a matter of fact.'

'I can explain,' Erm piped up nervously.

'I'm sure you can. And to think . . .' he leaned forward and eyed Nat reproachfully. 'the monk guy's directions were spot on.' Still leaning forward, he turned his head to look reproachfully at Erm. 'And you'll be pleased to hear I didn't consider it warranted a mention to Buzz. Instead, I thought a few well-chosen words directed into my newly-promoted boss's ear might do the trick.'

'But you don't understand?'

'Too true! I don't understand how you thought you could ever get away with it.'

'We weren't trying to get away with anything. All we were after was that piece of the action Buzz refused to give us, and you have to admit, what he wanted me to do isn't what you'd call crime-busting work, either. I regret things got out of hand.'

'No regrets, Erm. Without you two's noble efforts, I'd have been climbing up the wall by now.'

She looked relieved though with a puzzled expression on her face. 'I don't get it, Nat,' she said. 'Why didn't the monk believe I was in charge?'

'Out of uniform and attired in your present top and skirt, I imagine it could raise a modicum of doubt in some peoples' minds.'

'A lady Chief doesn't have to be a frump, does she?'

'I couldn't agree with you more. But you mustn't blame the monk for failing to detect the policewoman out of uniform. Didn't you notice how enamoured he was with you?'

'I thought he hardly noticed me.'

'Believe me...he noticed. And whilst on the subject of the monk, I would like to mention in passing how it didn't help much to convince him of your standing in the public domain when after requesting a sight of some official identification, and after much delving on your part into the various recesses of your new handbag, all you could come up with was a pair of handcuffs.'

'That's not my fault, Nat. I'm just not used to carrying a handbag and having to cope with all those bits and bobs one's supposed to carry in it. I had to look the part, didn't I? a normal kind of a girl carrying a normal kind of a handbag filled with normal kinds of things. *And* I had all my official gear in it as well. The gun, the badge, the cell-phone, those handcuffs, my ID - you know, the one I couldn't find - and a spray thingy pop insisted on me carrying when he spotted us at the park gates. He said it'd help to ward off undesirables. He's such a worry guts.'

'Your father was only thinking of your well-being, in case the usual kick in the groin fails to impress.'

'I can tell you for sure my usual kick in the groin never fails to impress.'

'Watch out!' warned Spencer. 'The monk guy's coming round the far bend. Before he gets here, I'd like to know exactly what he's been told and why Erm made out she was the officer in charge of the case?'

'At the time,' Nat informed him, 'it seemed the best way of handling it. Constantine already suspected Caleb of being an impostor and as soon as we heard where they intended to meet, we knew it'd be much more difficult to extricate the monks by getting Buzz's bunch of phoneys to change places with them. To start with there's no convenient convenience close by and no proper cover. The hides themselves are spread out around the lake and are too far apart to be of much use. We concluded the safest bet was to let Constantine into our secret and confirm what he already suspected that the present Caleb wasn't their true brother. We kidded him into believing he was a fugitive on the run. As one would expect, he wanted to know what happened to the real Caleb and we said we knew where he was, which was perfectly true, and that we would explain later. As for providing the new radio and refreshments, we told him the man was mad keen on baseball, which was also perfectly true. As the monk's eyes were glued on Erm and to keep him in a co-operative frame of mind, we thought that a little white lie would be in order. Trouble is, one little white lie led to another and before we knew it, Erm was running the show.'

'And what did you tell him about Buzz?'

'Nothing. It never came up.'

As Constantine was within earshot, the three rose to welcome him.

'This is Spencer Wright.' Nat introduced him.

'You mean, Sheriff Wright, don't you, Officer Foskett? We spoke on the phone, didn't we Sheriff? And I see you are also in disguise.'

'Eh?'

'Isn't a Sheriff usually in uniform?'

'I can see you're a monk guy who never misses a trick.'

'Mind you, it's nowhere near as good as your Chief's disguise. It fooled me completely.'

Erm whispered to Nat out of the side of her mouth. 'What's he mean by that?'

Nat whispered back out of the other side of his mouth. 'I'm certain it's meant as a compliment. Remember? He thought you looked too young and attractive to be the officer-in-charge.'

Her quizzical expression was replaced by an appreciative smile directed at the monk.

'And 'tis good news I bring you, Captain Kramer.'

Spencer's sharp intake of breath made Erm's smile disappear and it forced Nat into prodding her into a response. 'How nice!'

'Yes, isn't it. At this very point of time, you'll be pleased to hear your fugitive is with my fellow brothers in one of the hides. It was the only one unoccupied. Regretfully, it has a large gapping hole in the roof and the graffiti forces us to keep our eyes down on the floor.'

'What a shame!'

'Yes, isn't it. But at least with hardly any roof, our hide is filled with sunshine, not that your fugitive seemed aware of it. He was more interested in the graffiti. We all noticed.'

'The graffiti?'

'No, the way your fugitive behaved. Though I must admit the graffiti's somewhat difficult to avoid. It's on every wall.'

'With hardly any roof,' Nat observed, 'I imagine the floor is the only safe place left to cast an eye.'

'You might well think that, Officer. But the floor's covered in drawings of young ladies, stretched out, unattired. Casting an eye is one thing but knowing where to put one's feet is quite a different kettle of fish.'

'Just as well monks wear sandals,' Spencer observed.

He produced a local map from his pocket and asked the monk to pick out his hide.

Constantine was only too pleased to oblige and studied the map carefully before placing the tip of his finger on the spot. 'There it is, Sheriff. As you can see, it's quite secluded, and although I shouldn't ask, I suspect the impostor's original offence was one of duplicity. He struck me as that kind of man.'

Erm shook her head. 'I only wish I could spread the dirt, but I can't.'

'I fully appreciate confidentiality is of the utmost importance in your line of work and I will not embarrass you further by pursuing the matter. As Captain, I'm sure you know best. One doesn't become Captain by chance, does one?' He chuckled at the thought. 'But to get back to your fugitive, if you're planning to arrest him inside the hide, one would be quite willing to do one's duty by quitting the place even if it means missing all or part of the commentary on the ball game.'

'Thanks! We'll let you know,' Erm told him, 'as soon as we've worked out what's what. Meantime, would I be right in thinking you've filled the other monks in as to Caleb not being *your* Caleb.'

'Definitely not! Your instructions to keep my mouth shut were most explicit. No one, *but no one*, has been told.'

'What!!' Spencer exploded. 'How-the-hell-eck is that going to help?'

She whispered back out of the side of her mouth. 'I told him to keep his trap shut, but I only meant regarding Caleb and any outsiders, not his own buddies.'

'Is something wrong?' the monk inquired innocently.

'No! Nothing we can't handle.'

'If anyone can, I'm sure you can, Captain Kramer, especially when the answer's so self-evident.'

'Is it? I mean, it is!'

'One cannot let such an opportunity go begging to allow you and your men to enter the hide and arrest your scallywag whilst we - that is, my true brothers and I - are answering the call, unless...' the monk let out a snigger, 'he too, is otherwise engaged. In which case, you can apprehend him on his way out.'

Erm stared at him nonplussed. 'The call?'

'Of nature! What with all the drinks likely to be consumed, bearing in mind our usual intake is zero, it's an absolute certainty that none of us will last long into the ball game before necessity compels us to make a speedy exit. That's the excuse I gave to come here. As it happens, the nearest one is our usual one. Handily placed for you three by this seat, though not so handily placed for those of us on the other side of the river.'

'That means we can still make use of Buzz's monks,' Spencer hooted gleefully.

'Buzz, Sheriff? Who is Buzz and who are his monks?'

The other two winced at Spencer's lack of discretion. Though it allowed Nat to summon up all the creativity that a professional adviser can muster at a moment's notice. After all, he thought, if the great Lord Byron tells us a lie is "but the truth in masquerade", how can he, a mere mortal, reason otherwise.

'It's a codeword,' he told the monk, 'for our back up squad, B for Back and U for Up, you see, with Z for Zetetic and Z for Zone, refers to the squad allotted to our operational area.'

'And what about the squad's monks?'

'By an odd coincidence, your monastic designation in the plural happens to be the first letters of the name given to a technical computerised instrument used by Buzz. It's their "Measured Operational and Notational Kaleidoscopic Sensor".'

'Fancy that! What does it do?'

'Do? You'd be surprised as to its versatility. I know I am. It does all sorts of things. Very high-tech, you know.'

He held a hand to his brow as he concentrated his mind on coming up with a further load of technical bullshit. 'For example..' he clicked his fingers. 'at the touch of a button its kaleidoscopic sensor is immediately called into action ready to measure any operational and notational matters in urgent need of investigation. By chance, Sheriff Wright is a bit of a whiz-kid in the sensorial field and I'm sure he can explain its functions a lot better than I can.'

Spencer glowered as he tried frantically to think up an answer. 'If only we had the time to go into it,' he said. 'But duty calls and I must make a phone call.'

'You mean, about Buzz's Monks?'

'I can see there's no pulling the wool over your eyes.'

Spencer moved a distance away from the others before prodding his mobile's buttons. He listened for the sound of Buzz's voice and on hearing it, began to fill him in. It didn't take long before Spencer was the one doing the listening.

Officer Foskett whispered into the Captain's ear that it might be as well if they did a bunk before the balloon goes up. Erm thereupon informed the monk that the two of them would escort him back to the hide and that Sheriff Wright would follow on later. By the time Buzz finished conveying his thoughts to Spencer, the three were well out of sight.

On the way, Erm urged Brother Constantine not to do anything that might alert the impostor, Caleb, to their presence. And should he feel the need, on no account should Constantine or any of the other monks go along with him. And to make sure Caleb leaves the hide on his own.

Their walk took them passed numerous symmetrical and colourful flowerbeds set on either side of the path, on through a leafy bower covered with sweet smelling honeysuckle and eventually up to the steps leading to a pedestrianised bridge built across the Big Rock River.

Once on the bridge, Nat stopped for a welcome breather. He made out he was keen to admire the view. Erm made out she believed him. And the monk was pleased to join in. The three leaned over the parapet's wrought iron railings to gaze at the waters below. They twinkled ever changing in the reflected light of the sun. The effect was only broken here and there by splashes of froth created by rock-like obstacles sticking out through the water. They could see the many visitors dotted along the park's pathways on either side of the river. Here and there, the paths met or criss-crossed each other.

Across the bridge, the lake spread out before them like a rippling carpet of blue. It was surrounded by various shades of the browns and greens of trees, grass and bushes. On the near side of the park, the shades of browns and greens covered a much wider area. Contained within it, were numerous circled, oblong, and square patches of flowers and flowering shrubs of every conceivable colour. It was truly a magnificent sight.

Nat and the others were greatly impressed. They continued to drink in the view until they heard the sound of footsteps. Brother Constantine was the first to turn his head and as his eyes met the eyes of one of his compatriots, he let out a gasp. Instinctively, he placed a hand over his mouth.

'It's your fugitive, Captain Kramer.' He spoke softly to Erm through his fingers. 'We must have passed him by when he was otherwise engaged.'

In an instant, Erm exerted her newly acquired authority to the full. She instructed Constantine to return to the hide and stay put there with his fellow monks until notified to the contrary. She told Nat to stay calm and under no circumstances to get involved. Constantine sidled away unnoticed as Warren Tate's eyes fixed themselves unflinchingly on Nat. Even with a beard to contend with, Nat could see recognition plastered all over his face. To Nat's credit, he pretended not to notice and continued to drape himself over the railings.

Erm waited patiently for Warren to draw level and when he did, she unleashed a ferocious kick into his midriff. It sent him reeling back against the bridge's metal railings and although his long, brown robes helped to shield him from the full force of the blow, they were also greatly hampering his movement. He bounced back and his attempt to lunge out at her proved the point. She sidestepped him with ease and delivered a karate chop to the back of the neck for his trouble. As he fell, a frantic hand grasped the strap of Erm's new handbag and brought her down beside him. The strap snapped in the process, sending the bag flying across the bridge.

Nat was too worked up not to get involved. He raised his foot over Warren with the intention of using it to hold him down. Warren was having none of it, he grabbed Nat's ankle and yanked him off his feet. It sent him crashing to the ground, although it did allow Erm sufficient time to gain the initiative. She scrambled back up on to her feet and leaned over Warren, grabbed an arm, and twisted his body face downwards. She stuck a knee between his shoulder blades, grabbing the other arm from behind.

She called out to Nat to get her cuffs from out of "that damned handbag", but as he crawled to where the bag lay, Warren wasn't prepared to hang around long enough for Nat to produce them. Instead, he rammed the heels of his shoes hard into the crook of Erm's back and knocked her off balance. It took him but a moment to break free. And in that moment he rolled over and back into an upright position in one single movement. Erm was swift to follow suit, but not swift enough. He ducked behind her and wrapped an arm around her neck and squeezed. Erm struggled for all her worth to break free. She aimed an elbow into his ribs and kept repeating the operation over and over again.

Returning with the handbag, Nat lifted it high in the air and smashed it down on Warren's head. He hardly batted an eyelid. Almost as a retaliatory gesture, he swung Erm off her feet and held her aloft.

'Stop it! Stop it!' Nat shouted at the top of his voice. The look Warren gave him was one of contempt. 'If you don't,' Nat threatened, 'so help me God, I'll kill you if it's the last thing I do.'

Whilst continuing to sink an elbow into him, Erm swung her legs to and fro like the pendulum of a grandfather clock. The movement made it hard for Warren to keep his feet and made it even harder for him to keep the pressure up on her throat. She wriggled a hand in between her neck and his arm and further reduced the effectiveness of the hold.

Nat opened up the handbag and desperately sifted through the contents until he found the object of his quest, the Sheriff's gift to his daughter. He raised the spray can in line with Warren's eyes and tweaked his nose with the other hand.

With a curl of the lip, the head spun round to face him.

'*Please* watch the birdie?' said Nat as he applied his thumb to the aerosol's button.

An agonising scream filled the air.

Warren covered his face with his hands and Erm landed in a heap on the deck. Nat slung the can, moved back several feet, took a long, deep breath, lowered his head, and geared himself up. He charged at him like a bull in a bullring. Warren struck the railings with a resounding crunch and for a while hung precariously over the top of them, though not for long. Nat dived down, grabbed his legs, and with a single heave, toppled him into the water. A second scream filled the air.

Nat turned and flung himself down beside Erm. 'Say something?' he pleaded. 'You must say something, partner, otherwise I won't know what to do.'

Her eyelids flickered. 'Why don't you try mouth-to-mouth resuscitation?' she whispered.

Though her voice was weak, her arms were strong as she wrapped them around his neck.

'Like that?' he inquired after several minutes elapsed.

She nodded briefly and puckered her lips up for more. But their euphoria was soon shattered by the sound of a voice in its falsetto censure mode.

'What-the-hell have you two been up to?'

They recognised the voice immediately.

'I fear my attempts at mouth-to-mouth resuscitation . . .' Nat told her with a shrug of apology, 'may have come to an end.'

Erm glared up at Buzz disapprovingly. 'And he was just getting the hang of it, too!'

Chapter Twenty

Spencer's instructions were to undertake a search of a section of the Fortuna Valley estate's grounds. As he'd been particularly successful in discovering Warren Tate's precise location in the park, Buzz considered him to be the man for the job. Nat claimed he knew the estate like the back of his hand and was invited to act as guide. Spencer accepted his help with grave reservations. Erm was given the task of driving the patrol car. Having been personally congratulated by General Halstenberg on their success in putting Warren Tate out of action, the two suspected that the General had exerted pressure on Buzz to let them play a part. As it happened, a minor role suited them to a tee.

The car was heading down a stony track where the potholes were testing its suspension to the full. Erm parked it at the end of the track and suggested they should stretch their legs down a pathway running across the track and set between the bushes and trees. The pathway followed along the line of the chain-link fencing erected around the outer perimeter of the estate.

Spencer challenged Erm to provide "a damn good reason" why she'd parked the car on the outside rather than on the inside of the estate.

'We thought you might like to see this for yourself. It's the same path the two college kids were on the day they found the Doc's body.'

'But wasn't the body found inside, not outside the grounds?' As he spoke, Erm strode on ahead.

'True enough!' she called back at him. 'But we reckon what you're about to see is worth an extra special look.' She disappeared behind a clump of bushes and the other two followed on after her. 'This, Spencer,' she said, as she waved a hand at the open space in front of her, 'was reported to pop by the two high school kids. Connor checked it out and reported his findings to pop.'

'And I guess the Sheriff reported them to Buzz.'

'What do *you* think, Spencer?'

'About what?'

'The hole.'

'It's large enough for an elephant to get through, and as the rest of the fence is in good condition, Connor reckoned it was cut deliberately. Having seen it for myself, I'd say he was right.'

'Why d'you think no one noticed it before?' Erm asked Spencer.

'It's not obvious from the outside.'

'But it is from the inside.'

'Maybe it's off the beaten track as far as those inside the grounds are concerned. That's why the fence was cut where it was cut.'

Even though there was no semblance of a path inside the grounds, Nat cast doubt on Spencer's conclusions. But there were no doubts in his mind regarding the hole's cabbalistic connotations.

Spencer's mouth dropped. 'Wha-a-at?'

'Do you not agree it's likely to be the secret entrance and exit used by Warren?'

'Oh, that! Buzz reckoned it was a possibility.'

'And yet, surprisingly, Buzz has made no effort to delve deeper. Let's go through the gap and make our way to the summerhouse, shall we? You will notice the absence of security cameras en route. And later,' Erm announced, 'when we take the path from the summerhouse to the house itself, you won't find a single camera trained in our direction. Don't you think that's a mite odd?'

'More than a mite odd, I'd say. I guess Nat checked out the bank of VDUs at the house.'

'As a resident of Fortuna,' Nat said, 'it would have been easy for me to do so, but as it might have raised an eyebrow or two and an awkward question or two, I considered it would be better, and much more discreet, for me to survey the route on foot from the house to the summerhouse and on to the fence.'

Once inside the summerhouse, Erm invited Spencer to sit down on one of its fitted bench-type seats. She and Nat seated themselves on either side of him. Erm reminded Spencer that in most cases of homicide the murder weapon was dumped soon after use.

'And this case is unlikely to prove the exception,' said Erm.

'What makes you think that?'

'It's a kind of feeling we have deep down inside.'

'And I've also got a feeling deep down inside.'

'What kind of a feeling?'

'One that keeps on telling me that you two must be hiding something again.'

'As we've a notion as to the identity of the person who killed Caleb,' said Erm, 'it's not so much hiding something as doing something to show our appreciation for not letting on to Buzz. What we would like to do is to arrange for you to get the kudos for bringing the killer to book.'

'Oh, yeah? Pull the other one!'

Nat crossed his fingers behind his back and assured Spencer that their offer was genuine.

'Also,' Nat added, 'we're conscious of the fact that we might have been instrumental in causing a rift between you and Annie. Naturally, we'd like to make amends on that score as well.'

'You mean, about your suggestion to plump for Bartholomew in Annie's book as Jonquil's secret lover?'

'We're terribly sorry,' said Nat.

'No need to be. Although it turned out to be the guy called Kirk. As luck would have it, Bartholomew was Annie's choice as well.'

'*Nevertheless*,' said Nat, showing signs of irritation, 'our consciences wouldn't let us rest if we didn't offer you something. What do you say, Spencer?'

'If your offer's genuine, OK! Meantime, I'll wait and see what, if anything, you're able to deliver.'

Nat thought that was fair enough.

'So why not find out how good our delivery service is,' suggested Erm, 'by letting us guide you in the right direction?'

'As long as this time it *is* in the right direction.'

'Why not judge for yourself as we consider the facts together? Apart from Nat, Annie and Bennett, the only other person known to be absent from Fortuna at the time of the murder was the gardener, Oliver Jupp. The lawyer, Max Goldbloom, had a notion as to what became of Oliver but decided to wrap it up in a poser for Nat to solve as an old English definition of a hostel for travellers.'

'At first, it failed to click,' Nat told him. 'Then suddenly it hit me. In olden times, such hostels were noted for their hospitality. And for hospitality, read the word, hospital. So what happened to Oliver relates to what happened to his aunt. She took a turn for the worse and as a result, finished up in hospital. That's where Oliver was on the day of the funeral and on the day the will was read. He was at the aunt's home - where he spent the night and other nights thereafter - on the day Warren acted out his death scene. Unfortunately, I was convinced Oliver was implicated in the case. His absence at crucial times appeared significant. The fact that he always wore gardening gloves - Connor found a pair of his old ones in the bushes - helped fuel my suspicions. Also, Oliver wore overshoes when digging. It kept his shoes clean but it also changed the size of his normal footprint. But the Sheriff told me Oliver's shoes, with or without his overshoes, didn't fit the footprint, and bang went my theory. In respect of the doctor's murder, Oliver and Bennett were sheltering from the rain together. As you know, it put them both in the clear.'

'And,' said Erm, 'when Nat was on his initial walk around the lake, he saw a man in a baseball cap who he thought looked familiar. At the time, Nat couldn't put his finger on it. Now he can.'

Nat gave her a wry smile and posed a question to Spencer. 'Can you work out who we're looking for?'

'Someone, I guess, who left the house unobserved.'

'That being the case, may I suggest you cast your mind back to the events that took place in and around the gazebo at the time when your eyes first lustfully locked themselves on to Annie's sylphlike figure and later witnessed the late Chester Cornell's un-sylphlike figure being pursued by his eventual killer. Let us imagine for a moment you are inside the gazebo with the doctor. The doctor is discussing "money problems" with you and is putting his point of view over pretty vehemently. He is arguing the toss, you are arguing the toss, but he's in a strong position. He doesn't need your say-so to withdraw the money from the bank. In the end, he sticks two fingers up at you, tells you to get knotted, and bids you a fond farewell. What do you do?'

'I give chase and teach the bugger a lesson.'

'But do you wait a few seconds before giving chase?'

'Hell, no! I'm after him like a shot.'

'Then why did the doctor's eventual killer wait a few seconds before springing into action?'

'I guess he couldn't have been all that worked up about it.'

'In that case, why bother to give chase at all?'

'Something must have happened in those seconds to make him

change his mind.'

'What, for instance?'

Spencer thought for a moment or two before snapping his fingers. 'The killer was looking down at the Doc through the glass in the door and saw him send Annie crashing to the ground.'

'Bingo! You should bear in mind only the doctor's voice was sufficiently raised for Annie to hear what was being said. His companion was much more subdued and I would think more in control until Annie was unceremoniously shoved down the slope. At the bottom of the steps, there was a short period of hesitation as if the pursuer was torn between the doctor and Annie. Unluckily for the doctor, he won.

'Who is it, Spencer?'

'I guess it must be someone who likes Annie.'

'And who might that be?'

'Much as I'd like it to be, it can't be Bennett. The Jupp guy's in the clear, and it can't be the Cadogan woman, either. If she were in on it, she'd have kept her mouth shut and not told the Jupp guy anything about the Doc impersonating you in the bank. So it has to be . . .?' His voice tailed off.

'Someone expert with a gun?' urged Erm. 'The rifle used to kill Caleb and a handgun used to kill Craig. If you put the right question to pop, he'll confirm who it is without even realising it. Not like Nat, though. He became suspicious after Max Goldbloom's reading of the will.'

'But there was nothing in the will to point the finger.'

'Oh, yes, there was.' Nat was keen to enlighten him. 'The question I asked myself at the lawyer's office was, why was one of the members of Warren's staff left a bequest in the will, when at the time the will was made that person had yet to become a member of staff? Answer: that person was, and still is, a member of a particular gun club. Guess which club it is, Spencer?'

'I reckon it must be the Tate guy's club.'

'And it's the Sheriff's club as well.'

Spencer looked thoughtful as he eyed them for a time in silence.

'Other than for the Doc,' he said, 'the odd thing is that no one is able to verify the fact that Rosie Witherspoon was ill in her room when the murder of Caleb the monk took place. I guess the Witherspoon woman must be our man.'

Erm patted him on the back. 'You've almost cracked the case.'

'Almost?'

'You've yet to find the murder weapon.'

'And that's . . .?'

'And that's resting somewhere underneath your butt.'

Spencer sprang up like a jack-in-the-box.

'What the blazes are you on about?'

'What Erm is trying to say,' Nat informed him, 'is that the knife will be revealed once you've taken the trouble to lift up the upholstered hinged top. And that will happen after I've taken the trouble to unlock it.'

As Erm and Nat rose to join Spencer, Nat produced a key from his pocket. He thrust it into the covered keyhole in the side of the seat and gave it a quarter turn, allowing Spencer to lift up the hinged top. Underneath, it revealed a long compartment filled with cutlery of all shapes and sizes. A large carving knife rested across the top with its blade covered in what appeared to be dried blood. Spencer opened his jacket and from it produced a plastic bag and a rubber glove. He placed the glove on his right hand and carefully lifted out the knife and dropped it into the bag.

'Where did you find the key, Nat?'

'It's usually kept on a hook in the kitchen. As soon as I heard where and how Chester Cornell died, I slipped it into my pocket when no one was looking. Fact is hardly anybody takes the trouble to lock the various seat compartments. One key fits them all. Apart from the cutlery, the other compartments house crockery and glassware, as well as a variety of pots and pans.'

Spencer scratched his head as he gazed around the summerhouse.

'But where on earth can they be used?'

'Hidden behind the wooden panels at the far end are ceramic rings, a built-in oven, freezer, fridge and a work surface...a veritable Aladdin's cave for any good cook. As and when required, the panels can be lifted out separately.'

'But what made you think the knife was here?'

'By process of elimination. When Chester Cornell ran down the steps of the gazebo, he was aiming for the hole in the fence. To avoid being picked up by a security camera his route took him passed the summerhouse. We know Rosie's expertise is in the handling of a gun, and that suggests she wasn't carrying one at the time. But for certain, she knew where to lay her hands on a knife. A thorough search was made of the area around the summerhouse, so she didn't dump it there. She didn't have time to hide it in the house as she'd just reached the steps of the gazebo when the ambulance men arrived. Likewise, she didn't have time to consign it to the waters of the lake. It was far too risky for her to keep it anywhere on her person, especially dripping blood, or to sling it away willy-nilly on her way back to Annie. Therefore the seat's compartment was the obvious choice. No doubt Rosie intended to dispose of it later. But I put the kibosh on that by locking the compartment. In fact, I locked all the compartments to give the impression it was some new directive and hopefully make her think she hadn't been rumbled. She must have had fifty fits when she found it locked and the key missing and she dare not ask where it was or who'd locked it. In a way, she was hoist with her own petard.'

'What are you going to do with the key, Nat?'

'Return it from whence it came and no one will be any the wiser. Meanwhile, Spencer, I suggest you phone Buzz and tell him what a clever sod you've been.'

'Though you've given me your reasons, I still don't get why you're both willing to let me take the credit? Come on, admit it, there has to be something in it for you?'

'I assure you,' said Nat, 'we're only too pleased to be of service.'

Erm's sly wink coupled with an equally sly grin did nothing to ease his misgivings. He felt like a turkey coming face to face with those engaged in the preparation of the cranberry sauce. He shivered involuntarily but managed to raise a semblance of a smile.

He wondered if there'd be anything for him to smile about by the end of the day.

Chapter Twenty-One

Two police cars were parked on the gravel driveway by the entrance to the house at Fortuna. Erm drove one of the cars for her father and Connor drove the other with Elmer in tow. Although Spencer's car was in the parking lot at the side of the house, he was nowhere to be seen. In the end, Spencer decided to allow the Sheriff to do the honours as far as Rosie was concerned.

When Erm and Nat first disclosed their plan to the Sheriff, he made it clear that should they come unstuck, he would disown both them and their hare-brained scheme. Withholding evidence *is* a criminal offence. But as long as they understood the risks involved, he was willing to turn a blind eye.

Spencer's failure to consider how his success in the solving of the case would go down with Annie brought about a sudden change of heart, though only after Erm had taken Spencer aside and outlined the likely consequences. At that point, he realised he was about to drop a clanger of immense proportions. Putting Rosie in the frame could well put his future in doubt with Annie. Also, if he made the arrest (or even looked as if he'd anything to do with it), it could amount to the same thing. If he was to retain Annie's affection, the only course of action open to him, he thought, was to lay the blame at somebody else's door.

Once the Sheriff delivered Rosie suitably cuffed into the back of Connor's patrol car, he left it to him and Elmer to do the rest. After that, he strolled over to where Erm and Nat were standing on the driveway, but instead of looking pleased at making the arrest, his brow was furrowed and his face dejected.

Erm couldn't make it out.

'We thought you'd be on a high, pop, getting in on the act.'

'Sure am!' he said, though his voice was unconvincing. 'Once I confronted her, Rosie was re-al co-operative. She opened up with ease. Told me how the Doc was meant to take his piece of the action out of the bank account opened in Nat's name - twenty big ones first and the rest after Warren left the country. He was up to his eyeballs in debt. Playing the tables, she reckoned. The guy who came with him when he opened up the bank account was there to make sure he was in a position to pay them back. But the delay to Warren's departure was the last straw. The Doc was happy to keep his head down but thought it was only a matter of time before he was spotted. Not by us, it seems, but by the men in search of their pound of flesh...his flesh, if he failed to come up with the rest of the money on time. And d'you know what? I found the original print of Caleb; the one showing Hank in his barbershop days, in the drawer of her room. She hadn't even taken the trouble to destroy it. That's how sure she was of getting away with murder.'

'And what did Bennett have to say for himself?'

'Once he found out the extent, or more like, the lesser extent of his legacy, he underwent a change of heart as to who or who not to believe. Just as we thought, it was Warren who put the poison in on Nat. I tackled Bennett about the estate's lack of security cameras between the house and the summerhouse and on to the gap in the fence. He answered without giving it a second thought. Told me how Warren looked upon the summerhouse as a place to relax and to entertain his friends in private. With a strong chain-link fence protecting the perimeter, Warren insisted that security cameras were neither necessary nor welcome, and without his OK, the area was strictly out of bounds.'

'Doesn't matter how strong the fence is, pop, a gaping hole in it reduces its effectiveness a hell of a lot.'

'Sure thing! Bennett couldn't figure out what Warren was up to, and I couldn't let on.' The Sheriff suggested they should have a word with Spencer. 'Best try and ease him out, if you can.'

'We'll have a word with him later,' Erm promised.

'Why not now?'

"Cos he's in the conservatory trying to console Annie.' She cocked an ear. 'And not with much success by the sound of it.'

'OK! Leave it for the time being.'

'Anyway, Spencer's not likely to do anything untoward, pop, even if he thinks he's been hard done by. Having told Buzz he was the guy who found the murder weapon, he can't very well open his mouth up now and say he's made a mistake and it was Nat who really found it. It's just as well the knife was left where it was until after Warren Tate was put out of action, otherwise, we could have had Buzz and his men buzzing around the place, more than likely getting themselves noticed by you know who. In any case, Nat gave us a super demonstration of a crunch tackle, not that I saw any of it, mind you. Though I reckon the real crunch came when the waters parted and a submerged rock didn't.'

Nat blinked at her proudly. 'But without you, partner, I wouldn't have stood a chance.'

'Don't you mean,' the Sheriff pointed out, 'without my spray-can?'

'We all played a part in Rosie's capture. Just as well she wasn't set on going anywhere. At least, not whilst she thought Warren was still in the country.'

'But what I don't get,' questioned the Sheriff, 'is with *all* his money, why should he want to give it up to live in a communist state?'

'I'm not certain he intended to give it up,' said Nat. 'I wouldn't put it past him to try and have his cake and eat it. If he'd fooled us into believing he was dead, it would not only have given him the chance to flee the country undetected, but through his wife, Su Jiang, retain his rights in Fortuna and in most of his other assets as well. That's assuming his wife was happy to go along with it. I imagine she may have had other ideas of her own. Mind you, when the mood took him, Warren was quite a charmer, especially where the ladies were concerned. To the envy and frustration of his fellow man, he had the knack of acquiring a never-ending supply of them at the drop of a hat; or at a drop of whatever other item of his clothing happened to turn them on. From what I know or have gleaned, the fair sex simply adored him. Apart from the doctor, who was in it for the money, all those implicated in the case were women. But whereas his conquests tended to do his bidding, in the case of his wife, I suggest that the boot was on the other foot.

What was it Warren treasured most of all? A nude statuette in his bedroom, carved out of wood.

What the lawyer failed to mention when relating the details of Annie's bequest was the fact that the woman who modelled for the statuette was Su Jiang herself. Yet when Warren and his wife have the chance to get together again, what happens? He is set on leaving the US never to return, whilst she seems set on coming back here to claim his fortune. Odd, don't you think? On one occasion, I remember seeing Warren through the half closed door of his bedroom with the figure of his wife clutched to his chest and tears streaming down his cheeks. That wasn't the Warren I knew and laboured under. This Warren was showing emotions hitherto unheard of, and if I hadn't seen it for myself, I wouldn't have believed it. Later, when the opportunity presented itself, I inquired as to the current situation regarding his marital status, I told him that I needed the information for tax purposes, he gave me short shrift. They were still married, she was living abroad, and that was that. However, he did let out that over the years they'd met on a number of occasions, though not in the US - nor in North Korea, as we might now suppose - but in one or other European country. Tell me, which one of them, if any, do you think has been brainwashed, Warren or Su Jiang? Or perhaps both of them?'

'Make your point, partner? I know you're going to anyway.'

'In my opinion, Warren stands out as the most likely candidate and all on his own, too. I appreciate his wife has yet to turn up, but as she's still due to inherit, I lay odds on she will. And when she does, I bet the authorities will have their work cut out trying to prove she had anything to do with Warren's attempted defection, or that she's been living in or anywhere near North Korea, or in the country of the major power Buzz was talking about.'

'Strikes me,' said Erm, 'she's got it made.'

'As has someone else I could mention.' Nat winked at her.

'What are you getting at?'

'Listen?' Nat cupped a hand around his ear.

'I can't hear anything.'

'Precisely, Erm. All's quiet on the conservatory front.'

'Shall we all go and have a peek?'

The Sheriff wanted none of it. He told them: 'Duty calls!'

Erm stared at his long face and asked: 'What duty?'

'Remember what happened when we last visited your gran? A nosey do-gooder of a carer offered to give her a day out by getting *us* to look after her. She's home now and by all accounts, kicking up a hell of a fuss.'

'Better go, pop. A killer is one thing but gran's quite a different matter.'

Erm gave him a supportive smile and as he moved off, she and Nat went to see what they could see through the conservatory windows. It turned out to be nothing other than for the blinds drawn across them. For a moment or two, they felt nonplussed until Erm stuck out a hand and tried the door. It wasn't locked.

'Come and join us?' Spencer called out as they entered.

Annie was sitting next to him on a wooden bench with her head buried in his chest.

'We've come to see how you're getting on?'

Nat peered at the back of Annie's head and awaited a response. None came.

'We're both fine,' Spencer assured him.

'I mean, how does Annie feel? We know she's a girl of great compassion and humility. It's a virtue the two of us greatly admire. An example to us all not to judge our fellow creatures whatever the circumstances.'

At that, Annie shot up, spun her head round, and looked daggers at him.

'What I've learnt of late is that those who flatter, flatter to deceive.'

'Eh?'

'Rosie's no better than Warren. He let me down. She's let me down. What Warren left her in his will was a really nice old Chinese vase, worth a bundle. Max rated it highly. All that Warren left me was some crummy old wooden carving of some odd-looking nude, not worth a bag of beans. *And* Max had the cheek to say Warren treasured it most of all. I ask you, who does he think he's kidding?'

'But we could hear your voice raised as if you were upset?'

'That's 'cos I was upset as to how badly I've been treated.'

A smile lit up Spencer's face as he told them how pleased Annie was when she learnt how *he'd* managed to bring Rosie to justice. And as for the Sheriff (and everyone else, it seems), he emphasised the fact (quite a few times) that they were *all* acting under his instructions. He made it clear that he *knew* how to delegate. And he trusted his troops enough for them to do the donkey work whilst he was otherwise engaged.

The look on the other two's faces were enough to ensure Spencer's smile would last not just to the end of the day, but for many, many days to come.

Epilogue

Arlington was having one of its ceremonial days. The military were performing in the presence of the top brass and Erm and Nat were present by special invitation.

'Frankly, I'm disgusted,' said Nat.

'What they're doing *is* disgusting.' Erm echoed his feelings.

'He was nothing but a low-down snake in the grass.'

'A traitor to his country.'

'A cold-blooded killer.'

'You can say that again.' Erm literally spat out the words.

'What's the point?'

'Why don't we do something about it?'

'Such as?'

'I'll leave it to you,' said Erm, 'but whatever you come up with, it'd better be good. We never even knew he was in the army, let alone a lieutenant colonel. After all, if they've the gall to give him full military honours, then we've the guts to show 'em the error of their ways.'

'Why don't we turn it into an international incident?'

'How?' said Erm.

'When the General comes over, I'll kick him where it hurts.'

'Best leave the kicking to the expert.'

'Why can't I do it for a change? You don't half know how to bruise a chap's ego.'

'Is that what you call 'em?'

'But it wouldn't be an international incident if *you* did it. You're American.'

'OK!' she conceded. 'If you must, you must. Just remember, keep your weight on one foot, lean forward as that makes it easier to swing your leg with your bodyweight behind it, and make sure he's within range.'

Out of the corner of her eye, she spotted the General. Nat followed her advice and placed his weight on to his left leg and braced his right leg for action. But the General was set on approaching Erm first.

'It's nice to see you, er . . . er . . .'

'Erm.'

'Erm. I believe congratulations are in order.'

'We had a great time in Honolulu, and as a twosome for the first time.'

The General turned his attention to Nat who was having difficulty in keeping his balance.

'Please forgive the charade, er-er..'

'Nat.'

'Nat. And please forgive Buzz for not confiding in you. He's got a hell of a lot on his plate right now.'

Nat began to wobble.

'My sincere good wishes on your-er . . .'

The General stuck his hand out for a handshake. Nat grabbed it for support.

'We didn't tie the knot, General.'

'You didn't?' The General looked surprised. And he was even more surprised when Nat carried on clasping his hand.

'No! Nowadays, it's like going to college. Will we make the grade? Will we stay the course? If we borrow, will it take a lifetime to repay?'

But as Nat was becoming less steady on his foot, the grip on the

General's hand was becoming more vice-like by the second. It prompted the General to yank his hand free. It rocked Nat back on his heels.

'As things stand,' said the General, as he flicked his fingers back to life, 'I've no option but to place your medal on hold, and I don't believe you're to blame. Needless to say, Buzz doesn't see eye to eye with me on that one. He was dead set on taking our man alive.'

'Was he *very* upset, General?' Erm inquired.

'Very!' The news made the two feel a lot more upbeat. 'And we're damn sure there's still another mole in our midst. Hence the elaborate subterfuge.' The General waved his other hand expressively at the top brass gathered together to pay homage to the late Warren Tate.

'Does Buzz suspect anyone?'

'What he or I or any of us suspect is of no concern of yours. Apart from it being top secret, you're in no position to judge.'

'I agree my knowledge *is* limited but if I had to put money on it, I'd say your missing mole is female and answers to the name of Josephine Kerr.'

'How the bucking broncos did you come up with that one?'

'If you recall, General, she was with Buzz and the others in the car that picked me up for our meeting.'

'And?'

'She had the cheek to swipe my map of the locality.'

The General almost swallowed his Adam's apple in astonishment. 'What's that damn-well got to do with it?'

'When she spotted it in my hand, she looked unduly concerned. I saw her slide it under her backside in the car, and to cap it all, she failed to divulge her thieving acquisition to Buzz or to any of the others. I'd call that acting suspiciously, wouldn't you, General?'

'Maybe! But why-the-hell should a local map be of any concern to her?'

'Because it detailed the area around the top of Big Rock Ridge. The way I was holding it up meant that she could see the surface outline of the Monastery on it, and her reaction was automatic. Why should she react in such a way unless she knew who was hiding up there?'

'I reckon you could be bang on target. I can tell you in the strictest of confidence that she *is* on our short list. I can't imagine what Buzz will think when I give him the good news.'

I can, thought Nat.

I can, thought Erm.

And between them, they savoured the thought.